TINY (*in a Sondheimian frenzy*):

What'd I do?
What'd I say?
Why did these boys
all go away?
I tried hard to be
who they'd want me to be
though most of the time
I couldn't help being me.
Was I too loud?
Too quiet?
Why work on the package
when there's no one to buy it?
Am I not enough of a gay?
Not enough of a guy?
My love life's a train wreck
so I might as well fly. . . .

ALSO BY DAVID LEVITHAN:

Boy Meets Boy

The Realm of Possibility

Are We There Yet?

Marly's Ghost (illustrated by Brian Selznick)

Nick & Norah's Infinite Playlist (with Rachel Cohn)

Wide Awake

Naomi and Ely's No Kiss List (with Rachel Cohn)

How They Met, and Other Stories

Love Is the Higher Law

Will Grayson, Will Grayson (with John Green)

Dash & Lily's Book of Dares (with Rachel Cohn)

The Lover's Dictionary

Every You, Every Me (with photographs by Jonathan Farmer)

Every Day

Invisibility (with Andrea Cremer)

Two Boys Kissing

Another Day

HOLD ME CLOSER:
The Tiny Cooper Story

A musical in novel form
(Or, A novel in musical form)

by David Levithan

a companion to the novel
Will Grayson, Will Grayson
by John Green and David Levithan

speak

SPEAK
An imprint of Penguin Random House LLC
375 Hudson Street
New York, New York 10014

First published in the United States of America by Dutton Books,
an imprint of Penguin Group (USA) LLC, 2015
Published by Speak, an imprint of Penguin Random House LLC, 2016

THE LIBRARY OF CONGRESS HAS CATALOGED THE DUTTON BOOKS EDITION AS FOLLOWS:
Levithan, David.
Hold me closer : the Tiny Cooper story / by David Levithan
pages cm
Companion book to: Will Grayson, Will Grayson by John Green and David Levithan.
Summary: "Larger-than-life Tiny Cooper finally gets to tell his story, from his fabulous birth and childhood to his quest for true love and his infamous parade of ex-boyfriends, in the form of a musical he wrote"
—Provided by publisher.
ISBN 978-0-525-42884-8 (hardcover)
[1. Gays—Fiction. 2. Dating (Social customs)—Fiction. 3. Love—Fiction. 4. Musicals—Fiction.]
I. Title.
PZ7.L5798Hm 2015
[Fic]—dc23 2014039368

Speak ISBN 978-0-14-751610-7

Printed in the United States of America

Edited by Julie Strauss-Gabel
Designed by Irene Vandervoort

1 3 5 7 9 10 8 6 4 2

For Libba,
who I would have star in every musical

and

For Chris,
who I would like to have sitting beside me whenever I see one

AN INTRODUCTORY NOTE
from Tiny Cooper:

Hold Me Closer is meant to be true. (Except for the part where people keep bursting into song—that's only true sometimes.) No names have been changed, except if the person got really annoyed or mad that I was writing about him and asked me to change it. That said, certain ex-boyfriends did not get to decide whether or not their names would be used. If they have a problem with that, they should have never dumped me in the first place.

Like myself, this musical is meant to be loud and spectacular, although there are also some quiet moments. People who don't understand musical theater (i.e., most of my family, and a good portion of the greater Chicago area) tend to think of it as being unrealistic. I disagree. Because what is life if not a series of loud and quiet moments shuffled together with some music thrown in? My point being: Before you put on any production of *Hold Me Closer*, whether it's in your high school auditorium or on Broadway, it's important to realize that the truth is sometimes quiet . . . and other times, it's loud and spectacular. You don't always get to choose which form it takes.

But I get ahead of myself. It's best to think of this as a one-man show that happens to have lots of other people in it. I know it's not going to be physically possible for me to star in every production—although please ask me first when you start the casting process. The musical has already changed slightly since its first epic production.

That's the thing about life and love—every time you take another look at them, there's something else that can be revised.

For now, let me just say this: My name is Tiny Cooper, and it's time to raise the curtain on my bombastic, baffling, and hopefully stupendous story.

CHARACTERS

(in order of appearance)

TINY COOPER, age zero to sixteen
MOM, Tiny's mother
DAD, Tiny's father
LYNDA, the cool lesbian babysitter
PHIL WRAYSON, Tiny's best friend (most of the time)
COACH FRYE, a jerkface
THE GHOST OF OSCAR WILDE, as himself
EX-BOYFRIENDS #1 THROUGH #17, on parade
WILL, EX-BOYFRIEND #18, the most recent and thus most important one
DJANE, Tiny's friend and the girl Phil Wrayson is in love with (without admitting it)
ENSEMBLE of townspeople, church choir members, baseball teammates, Pride parade participants, and such.

MUSICAL NUMBERS

ACT I

"I Was Born This Way" .... Tiny
"OH! What a Big Gay Baby!" .... Tiny, Mom, Dad, Ensemble
"Religion" .... Tiny, Mom, Dad, Ensemble
"The Ballad of the Lesbian Babysitter" .... Lynda, Tiny
"Hey, Whatcha Doing?" .... Phil Wrayson, Tiny
"Second Base" .... Tiny, Ensemble
"I Know It, But Why Can't I Say It?" .... Tiny, Ensemble
"Stating the Obvious" .... Mom
"What Do You Do?" .... Dad
"I Know This Can't Be Easy For You" .... Tiny, Dad, Ensemble
"Dude, You Couldn't Be Gayer" .... Phil Wrayson, Tiny
"The Nosetackle (Likes Tight Ends)" .... Ensemble
"What Is Missing? (Love Is Missing)" .... Tiny, Lynda, The Ghost of Oscar Wilde

ACT II

"Parade of Ex-boyfriends" .... Tiny, His 18 Ex-boyfriends
"I Like" .... Tiny, Ex-boyfriend #1
"The Size of the Package" .... Tiny, Ensemble
"Close to a Kiss" .... Anonymous Movie Star
"You're Wonderful! I Don't Want to Date You!" .... Ex-boyfriend #5
"Summer of Gay" .... Tiny and the Camper Chorus
"Don't Hit Send" .... The Ghost of Oscar Wilde
"Saving Myself" .... Tiny, Ex-boyfriends, Ensemble
"It Wasn't You" .... Tiny
"Drunk on Love" .... Phil Wrayson, Djane
"Something Else" .... Tiny
"Finale" .... Ensemble

ACT I

In a suburb outside Chicago, starting with Tiny's birth sixteen years ago.

ACT II

Same suburb, only now Tiny's dating.

ACT I, SCENE 1

It's a dark stage, and at first all you hear are murmurs, a heartbeat, and heavy breathing. Like, serious Lamaze. Then we see, in the middle of the stage, a large piece of paper showing two bare, spread legs, discreetly covered by a hospital sheet. The heartbeat gets louder. The breathing gets heavier and more frantic, like a dinosaur is sitting on Santa and tickling him at the same time. Finally, as it all crescendos, **TINY COOPER** *comes into the world, crashing through the piece of paper and entering spectacularly onto the stage.*

We are not going for realism here. He should not be naked and covered with amniotic fluid. That's gross. He should not be wearing a diaper. He's not into that. Instead, the person who emerges should be the large, stylish Tiny Cooper that you will see for the next two acts. To delineate him from Tiny at other ages, you should have him wearing a button that says AGE: 0.

Most babies come into the world crying or gasping or snotting.

Not Tiny Cooper.

He comes into the world singing.

Cue: Opening chords of **"I WAS BORN THIS WAY."** *This is a big, lively, belty number—because, let's face it, if Elphaba got to sing "Defying Gravity" at the start of* Wicked, *she'd be much, much happier throughout the entire show. Tiny has just fallen into the world—some would say he was pushed—and* *already he has a sense of who he is and what he's going to do. The music and the production value* must *reflect that. Sparkles, people. Lots of sparkles. Do* not *get stingy with the sparkles. The reason drag queens love them so much is that you can get them for cheap.*

TINY:

Hello, my name is Tiny Cooper . . . what's yours?
I've just been born and, man, it feels good!

Cue music.

["I WAS BORN THIS WAY"]

TINY:

I was born this way,
big-boned and happily gay.
I was born this way,
right here in the U.S. of A.

It's pointless for you to try
to pinpoint how I became
so G-A-Y.
From my very first swish inflection,
the rainbow curved in my direction.

I've got brown hair,
big hips,

and green, green eyes.
And when I grow up
I'm gonna make out
with guys, guys, guys!

Why try to hide it?
What good would that do?
I was born this way
and if you don't like it
that says enough about you.

If you find it odd,
take it up with God.
Because who else do you say
could make me shine this way?

All God's children wear traveling shoes
whether you've got flat feet
or twinkle toes.
I'm going to dance right into this life
and keep dancing
as it goes.

I was born this way,
big-boned and happily gay.
I was born this way,
right here in the U.S. of A.

It's pointless for you to try
to pinpoint how I became
so G-A-Y.

From my very first swish inflection,
the rainbow curved in my direction.

I've got genes that fit me well
and a spirit all my own
I was born this way—
The rest is a great unknown!

Really belting now.

I.
was.
born.
this.
way.

And I love.
the way.
I.
was.
born.

The rest
is a great unknown.
But I'm ready,
oh yes, I'm ready
to find my own!

If anyone is going to object to this musical, they will have left the theater at this point. Which is fine. That means for the rest of the time, you'll have a crowd that really gets it.

Tiny Cooper steps over to the side of the stage, confiding in the audience. The stage clears. The spotlight is on him. (You will need a very big spotlight.)

A note on the spotlight: It should be very clear from the beginning that this is Tiny's special place. I know plenty of people—like my best friend, Will, and my most recent ex (also named Will; long story)—who want to stay as far away from the spotlight as possible. But there are those of us who draw our power from those electric moments when everyone is watching, everyone is listening, and there is the most perfect silence you can imagine, the entire room waiting to hear whatever you will say next. Especially for those of us who ordinarily feel ignored, a spotlight is a circle of magic, with the strength to draw us from the darkness of our everyday lives.

The thing about a spotlight is that you have to step into it. You have to get onto that stage. I haven't been ready for a lot of things, but from early on, I was ready for this.

TINY:

I can't remember a time when I wasn't gay, although there were definitely times I realized it more than others. And I can't remember a time I wasn't huge—which pretty much erased hiding as an option. This was my normal—big and gay. I would have never thought there was anything unusual about it. Except that I didn't live alone on a dessert island. [*Misspelling intentional!*] No, there had to be other people around. And the reaction I got from some of them made me self-conscious.

You don't think babies can hear you. But you're wrong. They can hear you.

The spotlight returns to the center of the stage. **TINY'S MOM** *is wheeling a rather large, somewhat garish pink baby carriage.* **TINY'S DAD** *is walking beside her. The* **CROWD** *is made up of neighbors, all of them nosy, many of them judgmental. As they sing* **"OH! WHAT A BIG GAY BABY!"** *you should get a sense that they are both intrigued and disturbed by having such a big gay baby in their midst. As for Mom and Dad—they are alright with having a big gay baby, but they're tired, because having a big gay baby takes a lot of work. Not just because he wants to dance all night and demands milk shakes from his mother pretty much every hour, but because of the endless questions from neighbors and the "guidance" of family members who seem to think Mom and Dad have control over how big or how gay their big gay baby is.*

Mom and Dad can no more make me straight than they can make me short. There's this thing called biology, and it's calling the shots. Mom and Dad realize this. Others do not.

The tune here is an old-fashioned town-crowd melody—kind of like how the people from the town in The Music Man *might sound if Harold Hill had brought an infant homosexual to town instead of wind instruments.*

["OH! WHAT A BIG GAY BABY!"]

CROWD:

Oh! What a Big Gay Baby!
He must weigh twenty pounds.
Oh! What a Big Gay Baby!
Why is he making those sounds?

TINY

(*makes baby disco sounds, sort of like a gay dance club has opened on Sesame Street*)

CROWD:

Oh! What a Big Gay Baby!
Feeding him must be such work!
Oh! What a Big Gay Baby!
He only falls asleep to Björk!

MOM and DAD:

Possibly maybe . . .
Possibly maybe . . .

CROWD:

He prefers hot male nurses
and cries at ugly purses.
Has a booty and knows to shake it.
Has a pacifier and loves to take it.

Oh! What a Big Gay Baby!
Bedazzle the diapers and order them large!
Oh! What a Big Gay Baby!
Pimp his crib the size of a barge!

MOM and DAD:

Look at this Big Gay Baby of ours—
not something you read about in Dr. Spock.
Look at our Big Gay Baby—
not what we were expecting when we were
expecting.
Hello, dear Big Gay Baby,
you might have to run before you can walk.

CROWD:

Oh! What a Big Gay Baby!
We're not really sure how we feel.

MEN IN CROWD:

Be a man, boy! Be a man!

WOMEN IN CROWD:

That's our plan, boy! That's our plan!

CROWD:

Oh! What a Big Gay Baby!
Already the size of a giant T. rex.
Oh! What a Big Gay Baby!
So unimpressed by the opposite sex.

He dances to show tunes
and has cheeks round as full moons.
We wish he'd show some respect,
but with a Big Gay Baby, what can you ex—

MOM and DAD (*spoken*):

Shhh! He's sleeping!

CROWD

(*turning it into a lullaby*):

Goodnight Sondheim, goodnight June.
Goodnight faggot, goodnight room.

Welcome, Big Gay Baby!
You're going to find . . .
it's a helluva world!

ACT I, SCENE 2

Now Tiny is four. (If he's wearing a button, change it to AGE: 4.*) The carriage is wheeled offstage, and Mom and Dad return carrying a pew-like bench. They sit down on it, with Tiny in the middle. The chorus arranges itself behind them, in the formation of a church choir.*

Tiny looks a little uncomfortable between his parents.

TINY:

It wasn't very long before my parents introduced me to their religion. I was four, so I didn't know there was any possibility of questioning it. Plus, I wanted so much to fit in. I know that's the story of our whole lives, but it all starts here. More than anything else, we want to fit into our own families.

DAD:

Son, it's very important to me that you take this seriously.

TINY:

Yes, Dad.

MOM:

It's not to be questioned. This is how we were raised, and it's how we are going to raise you. It is *very* important to us.

TINY:

I understand, Mom.

MOM and DAD:

Good.

The music for **"RELIGION"** *should be . . . well . . . religious. Hymnlike and intense, as if sung by a true church choir. It must be sung very seriously, as if we're in a house of worship. I mean, not in a* Sister Act, *gospel-choir sense—these are* NOT *nuns led by Whoopi Goldberg. They are from Illinois. And not the gospel parts of Illinois. We are deep in the suburbs here.*

Tiny looks slightly uncomfortable in the pew.

["RELIGION"]

DAD, MOM, and CHORUS:

Every Sunday
Every Sunday
Every Sunday
is our day
for religion.

Every Sunday
Every Sunday
Every Sunday
we congregate
and pray.

Every Sunday
Every Sunday
Every Sunday
is a
visitation.

Every Sunday
Every Sunday
Every Sunday
we watch
them play.

A television is wheeled out in front of the Cooper family. Dad turns it on. They are basked in the glow of the game. All the chorus members take out Chicago Bears banners and foam #1 fingers and begin to wave them in a synchronized, still church-like way.

As the song goes on, we should see Tiny getting more and more into it.

DAD, MOM, and CHORUS:

Hail Mary
Hail Mary
Hail Mary . . .
Pass!

Godspeed
Godspeed
Godspeed . . .
To the end zone!

(Hymnlike, the chorus now splits into men and women, echoing each other.)

WOMEN:

Remember the Super Bowl Shuffle.

MEN:

Remember the Super Bowl Shuffle.

WOMEN:

In this land of plenty—

MEN:

In this land of plenty—

WOMEN:

—we won Super Bowl Twenty.

MEN:

—we won Super Bowl Twenty.

WOMEN and MEN together (*in crescendo*):

Ditka!
Ditka!
Ditka!

(For those of you who prefer to avoid sports at all costs, Mike Ditka was not only a player when the Chicago Bears won the national championship in 1963, he was the head coach when they won in 1985. This is like Bernadette Peters winning a Tony for Song & Dance *in 1985 and then coming back in 2007 and winning for directing a revival of it. Which didn't happen, but I wish it had.)*

As Mom, Dad, and the chorus silently cheer on the Bears, Tiny speaks from the bench (aka our den's lime-green couch):

TINY:

I fell into my parents' religion not because it was required, not because they forced me into it, but because they invited me in and showed me the beauty of it, the faith it required, the devotion a person could give to something outside of himself. During that magical stretch from September to January, we would enclose ourselves in game time, watching the intricate, spontaneous choreography of each face-off, either on television or in the stadium itself. Only a nonbeliever looks at football and sees brute strength. A believer can see all of the layers—the strategy, the teamwork, the individual personalities clicking together. You can only control the game so much from the bleachers, so loving this game means having to give yourself up to the unpredictable, the unknowable. Your heart is bruised with every loss, but it's never broken. You sing with invincible joy at every win, but you're still vulnerable when the next game comes. My parents taught me all this, sometimes by telling me, but mostly by example.

Tiny now joins in with the song.

TINY, DAD, MOM, and CHORUS:

In the cold,
in the wind,
we'll be there for you.

Your agony,
your ecstasy,
we will feel it.

For four whole hours
there will be no other cares.
Just the sound of the play-by-play
of what happens to our Bears!

DAD (to TINY):

You throw the ball and hope.

TINY (*repeating, learning*):

You throw the ball and hope.

DAD (to TINY):

You catch the ball and run.

TINY (*repeating, learning*):

You catch the ball and run.

MOM and CHORUS:

As you gather on the field,
we will gather in our homes.
And we will pray.
Yes, we will pray.

(TINY and DAD join in.)

Every Sunday!
Every Sunday!
Every Sunday!
And sometimes Monday!

Try as hard as you can to convey what it's like to be together on a Sunday with your family, watching the Big Game. This might seem like a superficial number in the overall context of Tiny Cooper's life, but I assure you that it is not. The purity of his parents' belief—even if it's in the name of football—is one of the guiding lights for Tiny, and enables him to do all of the things he's about to do. He won't grow up to be a Bear himself (well, not in a football sense), and in truth, as his musical pursuits take hold, there will be Sundays when he will skip watching the game because of a badly timed matinee. But still he's taking the energy that was generated in these early days and using it to find his own religion, which will serve him well, even if at times it's confusing beyond belief.

Tiny's parents don't know it and will never understand it, but they're his role models.

ACT I, SCENE 3

The chorus members leave the stage, with Tiny remaining on the bench, still flanked by his parents.

TINY:

My parents kept me sheltered, protecting me from the haters that were out there in the world. I was my mom and dad's favorite thing, and this was always clear to me. But the older I got, they couldn't be there all the time.

DAD:

I have meetings.

MOM:

So many meetings interceding. I have functions.

DAD:

So many functions we can't function.

MOM:

We're committed to commitments.

DAD:

So committed to commitments.

On the bench, Mom and Dad start to pull away, doing other things. Tiny changes his button so it reads AGE: 5.

TINY:

Because of my size, everyone always thought I was older than I really was. The kindergarten teacher actually tried to turn me away on the first day of school. She probably would've served me a vodka tonic if I'd asked for one. But even though my body had grown, my heart and my mind were still the age they were supposed to be. And as my parents drifted further and further away, other people came into my life.

Mom and Dad leave the bench. **LYNDA** *appears in the wings. She is dressed like a very cool, down-to-earth sixteen-year-old girl.*

TINY:

The first close relationship I had with anyone outside my family was with Lynda, my lesbian babysitter. I have no idea if my parents knew she was lesbian or not. I have no idea if *I* knew what that meant at the time. All I knew was that I *worshipped* Lynda. To me, she was everything that adulthood stood for . . . making phone calls, knowing what was on TV, *driving a car.* To me, sixteen seemed like the *height* of adulthood. And every now and then, Lynda would let me get close to it, to see what it was really like.

LYNDA:

Who's my favorite guy?

TINY:

I am!

LYNDA:

And who will you never date?

TINY:

Jerks and assholes!

LYNDA:

That's right.

Lynda sits down next to Tiny on the bench. Even though Tiny sees her as being effortlessly old, she's really just a sixteen-year-old girl dealing with everyone's shit, including her own. The time she spends with Tiny is her escape from the outside world, and she wants to teach him a few things about life before she inevitably leaves him for Oberlin.

"THE BALLAD OF THE LESBIAN BABYSITTER" *is vulnerable and wistful, as if Joni Mitchell herself had come over for ten dollars an hour to share some world-weary wisdom with her big, gay babysittee.*

Bonus points if you can find an actress for Lynda who has hair long enough to sit on. She was that awesome.

Cue music.

["THE BALLAD OF THE LESBIAN BABYSITTER"]

LYNDA:

Come over here
and give me a hug
because my soul's been treated
like a threadbare rug.
Me and Heather
were meant to be forever,
but now she's into leather
and Red Bull dykes
who keep her out all night.

TINY:

Is there anything I can do?

LYNDA:

Just rub my shoulder
because I'm feeling so much older.
Rub my back
and drain me of the black that's left
when a relationship ends.

He rubs her back.

Now hand me my sketchbook
so I can use this pain
to pull my hopes
back out of the drain.
Watch carefully, Tiny,

how to disable your rage
by unleashing it onto
an empty page.

TINY (*to audience*):

It didn't matter that I was five—
I saw her pain come alive.
Just like a sorcerer
fighting a deadly foe,
she met it eye to eye
and wouldn't let go.

Drawing the girls who always hurt her,
sketching the loves as they'd desert her.
All the drama became less troubled
once the hard words had been inked and
  bubbled.

LYNDA (to TINY):

Look forward to the moment
when it all falls apart.
Look forward to the moment
when you must rearrange your heart.

It might feel like the end of the world—
but it's the beginning of your art.

Lynda sketches during an instrumental, then puts down the book, sighs, and sings the next verse to Tiny.

LYNDA:

Come over here
and give me a peck
because my faith in people's
a miserable wreck.

He kisses her cheek.

Me and Leigh
were meant to be,
but now she wants to flee
into the arms of a maître d'
at a boulangerie—
and she doesn't even like
to French.

TINY:

Is there anything I can do?

LYNDA:

Just rub my feet,
ease my defeat.
Rub my neck
so I'm no longer the speck that remains
when a relationship ends.

Now hand me my sketchbook
so I can use this pain
to pull my hopes
back out of the drain.

Watch carefully, Tiny,
how to disable your rage
by unleashing it onto
an empty page.

Are you listening?

TINY:

I am listening.

LYNDA:

Are you watching?

TINY:

I am watching.

LYNDA and TINY:

Look forward to the moment
when it all falls apart.
Look forward to the moment
when you must rearrange your heart.

It might feel like the end of the world
but it's the beginning of your art.

Lynda rips out a page and gives it to Tiny, who folds it carefully and keeps it. (He still has it.)

The song ends, but the advice continues. (He still remembers it.)

LYNDA:

Don't get trapped into thinking people are halves instead of wholes.

TINY:

People are halves?

LYNDA:

They're not trying to sell you on it yet, but believe me, they will. The idea that two is the ideal, and that one is only good as half of two. You are not a half, and you should never treat someone else like a half. Agreed?

TINY:

Agreed!

She hugs him. End scene.

ACT I, SCENE 4

As the stage goes dark (and the scenery is changed), Tiny steps forward, again in the spotlight.

TINY:

Having a babysitter and two parents in your corner is great—but what I really wanted was a best friend. I had plenty of friends—there was no shortage of birthday party invitations in *my* cubbyhole—but I had yet to find my co-conspirator, my co-adventurer, the right-hand man who I'd give my left arm for.

And then Phil Wrayson came into my life.

Now, I'm sure that I joined Pee Wee League because I wanted to play baseball. But soon I found that the best part of Pee Wee League wasn't the playing—it was all the time when we weren't playing, when we were just hanging around in the dugout or on the field. Phil Wrayson and I went to school together, but it wasn't really until Pee Wee League that we got to know each other.

At this point, a kid dressed as a batboy should walk out and give Tiny a baseball cap and a button that reads AGE: 8.

When the lights rise on the stage, it's been turned into a dugout.

Right now the only kid sitting there is **PHIL WRAYSON**, *deep in thought. An open book is in front of him, although he's not reading it. All the other players are on the field.*

Physically, there's nothing remarkable about Phil Wrayson. He's cute, but there's nothing striking about his cuteness. You can imagine hundreds of other guys who are just as cute. The thing about Phil is that he's a really good guy. I know that's hard to show onstage, but there's something about his goodness that needs to be conveyed. Again, it isn't striking—a guy who advertises his own goodness is just another kind of asshole. The goodness is just a part of who Phil is. He doesn't even realize it.

The cadences of **"HEY, WHATCHA DOING?"** *are very much the cadences of two eight-year-old boys—even if the vocabulary level may admittedly be heightened here for dramatic/comedic (cometic? dramedic?) effect. Tiny is trying his darnedest to start a musical conversation with Phil, but at first, Phil's not into it. Luckily, Tiny's persistent—like Angel in* Rent, *but without the cross-dressing and the specter of AIDS hovering over everything. By the end of the song, Tiny and Phil are friends.*

["HEY, WHATCHA DOING?"]

TINY (*sung cheerily*):

Hey, whatcha doing?!?

PHIL (*spoken, not looking up*):

Not much.

It feels like the song is over. The shortest song in the history of friendship. Phil starts to read the book in front of him, a little embarrassed to have been caught daydreaming. Tiny tries again.

TINY (*sung*):

Hey, whatcha reading?

PHIL (*spoken*):

I'm reading about snakes.

He holds up the book. It's about snakes. Again, it seems like the song will end here. But Tiny persists.

TINY (*sung*):

Hey, what's it saying?

PHIL (*spoken*):

About snakes?

TINY (*sung*):

Yeah, about snakes. Tell me everything I've
always wanted to know about snakes but was
afraid to ask!

PHIL (*spoken*):

Well . . . a lot of them are poisonous.

TINY (*sung*):

And?

PHIL (*spoken, warming up*):

The longest one ever in captivity was Medusa, a twenty-five-foot python.

TINY (*sung*):

And?

PHIL (*sung*):

And Medusa's diet included rabbits, hogs, and deer!

TINY (*beaming, and loudly sung*):

That's the coolest thing I ever did hear!

Phil seems surprised by this sudden burst of friendship. At this point, the other team members, all in uniform, come back and mill around. Phil's book disappears, and a notebook appears. The other team members leave, and Phil opens up the notebook.

All dialogue is sung from here on in, until end of song.

TINY:

Hey, whatcha doing?

PHIL:

I'm trying to get through math.

TINY:

Math was invented by a psychopath.

PHIL:

A psychopath who never takes a bath.

TINY:

A stinky, smelly psychopath—
that's who invented math.

Both boys are very proud of themselves and their repartee. But now there's an awkward pause. Until Phil unexpectedly (to both of them) jumps in.

PHIL:

Hey, whatcha doing?

TINY:

Just thinking, you know.

PHIL:

I know what it's like to be thinking.

TINY:

I'll be standing in the outfield, staring at the sky . . .

PHIL:

. . . but what I'm really seeing are the thoughts
that travel by.

TINY:

I pretend the clouds are in a soap opera . . .

PHIL:

I make friends with blades of grass.

TINY:

There are clouds in love, clouds in lust . . .

PHIL:

I'm afraid the coach will kick my ass.

Singing this line makes Phil downcast, and Tiny notices. The other players return, and again the stage is full with the comings and goings. Tiny steps downstage to address the audience.

TINY (*spoken*):

Phil became a decent first baseman. I found that my talents at basketball and football—two sports that appreciate size—were not transferable to the baseball diamond. Very quickly, I held the league record for being hit by pitches.

Nothing can cement a friendship like a common enemy. And in Little League we found that in a certain Fascist-forward despot named Coach Frye. I haven't changed his name, because I would love to see Coach Frye try to sue me. Bring it on, Coach Frye. There's not a jury in the world that enjoyed gym class.

Tiny sits down on the bench, itchy and restless. The other teammates sit on the bench, too.

COACH FRYE *comes out. He's ugly and out of shape. You know those gym teachers who force you to do ten thousand sit-ups even though they themselves haven't seen the lower half of their body in twenty years? The ones who blow their whistles like they're the master and you're the dogs? Yeah, that's him.*

COACH FRYE (*spoken*):

Alright, you pansies. I don't want you to sissy up the field, understood? This isn't a *softball* team—I want you unloading *artillery* out there. Billy, you're up.

One of the boys leaves the bench and goes offstage. The kids' eyes follow him. They start to cheer him on.

COACH FRYE (*yelling*):

Come on, Billy! Did your mom teach you how to hold a bat? This isn't *gardening*. Wait for your pitch and *don't just stand there.*

Then Tiny's cheer drowns out all the others.

TINY (*exaggeratedly effeminate, even flirtatious*):
Hey, batta batta. THWING, batta batta!

BULLY PLAYER #1:
Idiot. *Our guy* is batting. You're distracting him!

PHIL (*coming to Tiny's defense*):
Tiny's rubber. You're glue. Whatever you say bounces off him and sticks to you.

BULLY PLAYER #2:
Tiny's gay.

COACH FRYE:
Hey! HEY! No insulting teammates.

PHIL (*valiantly*):
It's not an insult. It's just a thing. Like, some people are gay. Some people have blue eyes.

COACH FRYE:
Shut up, Wrayson.

BULLY #1 (*loud whisper*):
You're so gay for each other.

PHIL:
We're not *gay*. We're *eight*.

BULLY #1:

You want to go to second base . . . WITH TINY.

TINY:

Second base?

Tiny stands up and takes a step downstage, in front of the coach, who seethes. **"SECOND BASE"** *is about to begin.*

This is Tiny's number, but everybody's going to be looking at the boys in uniform. This should be the most homoerotically charged baseball dance number since "I Don't Dance" in High School Musical 2. *As Tiny sings, the guys in the chorus—including Phil—pull off a hilariously elaborate old-fashioned, high-stepping, highly choreographed dance, their bats used as canes and their ball caps as top hats. Midway through, half the guys swing their bats toward the heads of half the others, and even though it's totally faked, when the other boys fall backward dramatically and the music cuts out, the audience is going to gasp. Moments later, they all jump up in a single motion and the song starts up again. (Or, if you can't do all that, just make it fun.)*

At first, Coach is startled. Tiny is taking over his team, winning them over with his song. Once he realizes this, he storms off.

At another point, Billy should probably run back from the batter's box and join in. We wouldn't want him to lose out on the fun just because he's up at bat.

The key thing here is that, as should be obvious from the lyrics, Tiny has no idea what he's talking about. He's not identifying as gay to his teammates—he's just asking a question. And it's clear that he has no answer. He hasn't thought about sex much. He's eight.

["SECOND BASE"]

TINY:

What's second base for a gay man?
If you can't tell me,
I'm hoping somebody can.
When I hit the field,
I want to know where to run.
Don't want to be tagged out
before the fun's begun.

What's second base for a gay man?
Is it tuning in Tokyo?
I can't see how that would feel good,
but maybe that's how it should go?

CHORUS:

Hey, batta batta!
Swing, batta batta!

TINY:

Is it spooning or sporking?
Parabulating or torquing?
Hot or cold, fast or slow,
holding close or letting go?

CHORUS:

Hey, batta batta!
Swing, batta batta!

TINY:

Is it carnal or karmic?
Pastoral or tantric?
Is it Ontario or Saskatchewan?
Eyeing Iceland or petting Pakistan?

Send the answer in a bottle
or beam it in from outer space—
just somebody please tell me
how a gay man gets to second base!

Largely instrumental interlude for homoerotic baseball dance number. Containing the refrain:

CHORUS:

Swing low, batta batta,
coming forth to carry us . . .
home!

Swing low, batta batta,
coming forth to carry us . . .
home!

TINY:

Do I glide to second base
or slide in headfirst?
Can I steal when no one's looking
or is that asking for the worst?

I've checked my Bible and skimmed Sedaris.
I've even consulted my *Deathly Hallows*.
Please please please—I haven't been to first yet
but I'd sure like to know what follows!

CHORUS:

Swing low!
Swing hard!
Swing low, batta batta!
Swing hard!

At this rousing finish, the audience will hopefully drown you in thunderous applause. Use this as an interval to clear the stage. Only Tiny remains. He should take his AGE: 8 *button off before he speaks.*

TINY:

Even if Phil didn't have answers to all of my questions, like the location of second base for a gay man, he still became the most important person in my life. In middle school, I ended up punching Coach Frye in the nose in Phil's defense. Meanwhile, Phil's defenses of me were a little more . . . subtle.

He was my best friend. But still there were some things we couldn't talk about.

Phil comes walking out onstage, wearing the clothes of his seventh-grade self. He gives Tiny a badge that says AGE: 12. *The following exchange is spoken.*

PHIL:

Hey, whatcha doing?

TINY:

Not much, what're you doing?

PHIL:

Not much. (*Pauses. Looks at Tiny.*) Look, Tiny. If you ever want to talk to me about boy stuff, you know you can, right?

TINY:

Boy stuff? Like snakes and airplanes and war?

PHIL:

No, like . . . boys. Just because I don't crush that way, it doesn't mean we can't talk about it. I mean, I groan about girls to you all the time.

TINY:

I have *no idea* what you're talking about. Did you see the Bears game last night?

Phil looks disappointed and leaves the stage. Tiny, meanwhile, turns to the audience.

TINY:

It's always easy to blame other people for holding you back. But sometimes, the only person holding you back is . . . well . . . you.

ACT I, SCENE 5

The batboy comes out and gives Tiny a new button, which reads AGE: 14.

TINY (*spoken*):

Sometimes a long, dark night of the soul can last for weeks, months, or even years. In my case, it was weeks, but still. Those weeks had years behind them. Because even though I was born gay, and grew up gay, and liked boys in that way and didn't like girls in that way, there was something holding me back: that one simple word—*gay*—spoken out loud.

It was a glass closet. Everyone could see me inside. I waved to them *all the time*. But I was trapped nonetheless. I had supportive parents, but I'd never really had the conversation with them. I had a best friend, but I'd never had the conversation with him, either. I'd never had a boyfriend. I'd never really tried. I'd lost myself in football, in school, in jokes and fashion. But by being lost in these things, I was losing myself.

I know it's hard to believe, but it took me a while to actually say it. Sometimes it's hard, even when it shouldn't be. And sometimes it's hard because it is.

That's what this song is about. Normally in a coming-out story, the big scene is when the main character tells his parents. Or his best friend. Or the boy he loves. But ask anyone who's ever been through coming out—and I'm not just talking about coming out as gay here, I'm talking all kinds of coming out. We all know: The first person you have to come out to is yourself. So this scene is just me alone on a stage. Because that's how it was. Me alone, singing to myself, and finally hearing it.

Piano, please.

Cue piano intro.

["I KNOW IT, BUT WHY CAN'T I SAY IT?"]

TINY:

Ever since way back when,
I've played with Barbies
and dreamed of Ken.

I've read *Vogue* from cover to cover
like an unrequited lover
waiting for his ticket
to the midnight ball.

My room is full of hoardings
of original cast recordings,
singing to me of somewhere,
and glory, and hope.

Even a blind man can see
what is going on with me . . .
but when I reach for the words
they're not there.

I know it, but why can't I say it?
Why am I hiding
the thing I know the most?
Who am I trying to be
when I'm denying I'm me?
Why is the truth
so stuck inside?

Hiding.
There's not much chance of hiding.
And still I'm not confiding,
afraid of something I can't name.

Careful.
I tell myself,
be careful.
But sometimes
careful
cares too much
about what people think

and what they might say
their careless remarks
about you being—

Tiny stops. He can't say the word. In the silence, the **CHORUS** *comes onstage. It is a chorus of gay kids—some of them the boyfriends from the second act, some of them young lesbians, including Lynda, the lesbian babysitter. One of them, to appear again later, is* **THE GHOST OF OSCAR WILDE**.

CHORUS:

I know it, but why can't I say it?
Why am I hiding
the thing I know the most?

TINY and CHORUS:

Who am I trying to be
when I'm denying I'm me?
Why is the truth
so stuck inside?

Hiding.
There's not much chance of hiding.
And still I'm not confiding,
afraid of something I can't name.

Careful.
I tell myself,

be careful.
But sometimes
careful
cares too much
about what people think
and what they might say
their careless remarks
about you being—

TINY:

gay.

There's a pause in the music as the word is felt. Tiny is both scared and exhilarated to have said it out loud. The chorus chimes in.

CHORUS:

If they're truly your friends, you won't lose them.
If they don't get it at first, you'll excuse them.
If they love you, they'll want you to love.
If they love you, they'll want you to be loved.

TINY:

I know it.

CHORUS:

So you must say it.

TINY:

I say it.

CHORUS:

Because it is your truth.

TINY:

Hiding.

CHORUS:

There is no meaning in hiding.

TINY:

Careful.

CHORUS:

Don't be careless with your heart.

TINY:

If they're truly my friends—

CHORUS:

—you won't lose them.

TINY:

If they don't get it at first—

CHORUS:

—you'll excuse them.
If they love you, they'll want you to love.
If they love you, they'll want you to be loved.

TINY:

I know it, and so I will say it.
No more hiding
the thing I know the most.
I am trying to be
the me I know I can be.
So starting today
I will be openly

CHORUS:

Openly

TINY:

Openly

CHORUS:

Openly!

TINY:

Gay!

At the end of this song, Tiny should look very relieved.

ACT I, SCENE 6

The lights go out. When they come back up, we've returned to the stage setup we saw in the "Religion" scene—this time Mom and Dad are sitting on the bench, and Tiny is in front of them.

For this number, Tiny speaks all of his lines, Mom sings hers, and Dad remains silent.

["STATING THE OBVIOUS"]

TINY (*spoken*):

Mom. Dad. I just wanted to let you know . . . I'm gay.

MOM (*sung*):

Oh, Tiny.
Our Tiny.
We know, Tiny.
It's okay.

TINY (*spoken*):

I dream of boys. I fantasize about boys. When I jerk off, I think of boys. I mean, not that I jerk off or anything.

MOM (*sung*):

The strongest kind of love
is unconditional love.

The moment you were born,
I knew unconditional love.

TINY (*spoken*):

And while I'm coming out, I might as well tell you that time I told you Djane must have stolen your lipstick when she was over? Well, that was me. But I didn't really like the way I looked in lipstick. At least not that color.

MOM (*sung*):

You are so complicated.
I can see.
But you're good at heart.
And that's what matters to me.

TINY (*spoken*):

I cheated at algebra. There's a reason your vodka tastes watered down. I feed my peas to the dog every time you serve them. I just don't want to hurt your feelings.

MOM (*sung*):

We'll always love our Tiny
And we'll always love your Tiny, too.
We can't wait to witness
All the big, gay things you'll do.

TINY (*spoken*):

I download porn on the family computer, but I

burn it to disk so it won't actually be on the hard drive. And you know how I told you I worked at the library at school to pay for my subscriptions to *Vogue* and *Details* and *Men's Health*? Well, that was actually the birthday money Grandma sent me that she wanted me to spend on my "religious education."

MOM (*sung*):

Look at this Big Gay Baby of ours—
not something you read about in Dr. Spock.
Look at our Big Gay Baby—
not what we were expecting when we were
    expecting.
But we love him.
Oh, yes, we love him.

TINY (*spoken*):

You're okay with this, aren't you? I'm not going to say I'm sorry. I'm not sorry. The only thing I'm sorry about is keeping it from you for so long. And maybe the peas, because I think Baxter likes them even less than I do.

MOM (*sung*):

Don't be sorry.
Never be sorry.
You don't have to be.
We love you.
We'll always love you.
Unconditionally.

Tiny and his mother embrace. Then Tiny looks to his father, who's crying. All dialogue is spoken here, to end of scene.

TINY:

Dad?

DAD (*trying to hide his tears*):

It's okay, son. Everything she said.

TINY:

Really?

DAD:

Really.

TINY:

Then I hope you don't mind . . . I signed us up to be in a mother-daughter fashion show. I thought that would be a great way for me to let everyone know who I am. Is that okay?

The spotlight closes in on Dad. He's caught.

ACT I, SCENE 7

Tiny's father takes center stage. As the scenery changes behind him to set up for the scene after this one, he opens up to the audience. He loves his son—there's no doubt that he loves his son. But still, this is hard for him.

["WHAT DO YOU DO?"]

DAD:

What do you do when your son
asks you to be in a
mother-daughter fashion show?

Do you pack up and leave
or figure out the best way to say
no, no, *no*?

It's a public display,
an embarrassing array
of all the things
you don't want people to say.

My own father took me fishing
and left me always wishing
that being in that boat
would make us less remote.

But instead we'd sit without speaking,

time together slowly leaking.
Our lines tied in a knot,
the big one never caught.

I told myself that when I became a father
I'd be the type who'd always bother.
I'd get to know my son.
Never scorn, never judge, never run.

In order to be a good father
you have to be a good mother.
You have to take every chance
as if you won't get another.

My father died
before I could ask the right questions.
Now I ask them anyway
and never get answers.

What do you do when your son
asks you to be in a
mother-daughter fashion show?

I'll tell you what you do—
You go.

As the audience hopefully applauds Dad and his decision, he goes offstage. The lights go up, and we see the runway for the mother-daughter fashion show assembled. Soon, mothers and daughters (all played by girls, just to make the juxtaposition more effective) are parading in matching outfits to the opening strains of **"I KNOW THIS CAN'T BE EASY FOR YOU."** *It all climaxes when Tiny and his dad appear . . . in matching outfits.*

A note on the outfits: This is not a drag show for Tiny and his dad. Even though there is nothing at all wrong with a boy wanting to wear dresses, there is *something wrong with assuming that every gay boy wants to wear dresses. Some might. Some don't. Tiny was never into that particular Cage aux Folles, so when he suggests his father and he participate in a mother-daughter fashion show, they are dressed the way he wants to be dressed—FABULOUSLY. Needless to say, there should be more sparkle and brightness than Tiny's dad has ever considered wearing. (Also note: There is also something wrong with assuming that every gay boy wants to wear sparkles and bright colors. Some don't. I do.)*

Tiny and his dad's entrance leads, of course, to a big production number.

Tiny is somewhat astonished that his father has agreed to do this with him. And Tiny's dad is very much astonished that he's at a mother-daughter fashion show. This isn't like the end of Grease, *when Sandy is suddenly liberated by trying on a slutty girl's clothes. Tiny's dad is very uncomfortable.*

What follows is a reflection of their emotions.

["I KNOW THIS CAN'T BE EASY FOR YOU"]

TINY:

I know this can't be easy for you.

DAD:

I won't try to deny that it's true.

TINY:

There are other ways of spending a Sunday . . .

DAD:

. . . than walking with your son down the runway.

TINY:

But here we are in matching outfits.

DAD:

Just look at where my waistline sits!

TINY:

Balls out with the family charm . . .

DAD:

. . . trying not to pull the nearest alarm.

TINY (*pause, then spoken*):

I'm really glad you're here.

DAD:

I know it can't be easy for you.

TINY:

I won't try to deny that it's true.

DAD:

There must be times when you feel like a target.

TINY:

Which is why I live my life like I'm totally jet-set.

DAD:

I just hope I'm a good father.

TINY:

I just hope I'm a good son.

TINY and DAD:

I never know—
I only know—
this can't be easy for you.

They head down the runway.

CHORUS OF ONLOOKERS:

I know this can't be easy for you.
Just hold your smile

and see it through.
Everybody's watching—
they always do.
Step forward
and forward
and never forget
the person standing next to you.

TINY:

In so many ways you amaze me.

DAD:

In so many ways you amaze me.

CHORUS OF ONLOOKERS:

I know this can't be easy for you.
But it can be so many other things too.

TINY:

So hold your smile

DAD:

and see it through.

TINY and DAD:

Together
we can do this.
You and I.
Here and now.

TINY:

You throw the ball and hope—

DAD:

You catch the ball and run—

TINY:

You walk wide—

DAD:

You walk tall—

TINY:

You don't hide—

DAD:

You don't fall—

TINY and DAD:

Step forward
and forward
and never forget
the person standing next to you.

They make it through. With style.

ACT I, SCENE 8

Tiny comes downstage again, to allow for the scenery to change.

TINY:

Next up was Phil Wrayson. In order to come out to him, I invited him to the Gay Pride Parade in Boystown. For those of you not from the Chicago area, Boystown is, well, the place in town where boys who like boys go to be boys who like boys and see other boys who like boys. You would think that this destination alone would have been my coming-out statement, but such is the logic of a boy coming out to his best friend that even at a Gay Pride Parade, the conversation needed to be had, no matter how nervous-making it was.

As Tiny is talking, the stage transforms into a Pride parade, complete with drag queens, leather daddies, gay parents, and (if you can fit them onstage) Dykes on Bikes. Phil Wrayson is right there with them, looking out of place, but not self-consciously so.

PHIL (*coming up to Tiny*):

I'm trying to imagine what the straight equivalent of this would look like.

TINY:

The morning commute?

PHIL:

I was just asked by a drag queen if I was into otters. I'm hoping she didn't mean that literally. That has to be a nickname for something, right?

TINY (*nervously*):

Phil, there's a reason I brought you here.

PHIL (*not getting it*):

I hope it's not to pimp me out to otters. Truly, I'm not into otters.

TINY:

Phil, I'm gay.

PHIL (*mock-stunned*):

No!

TINY (*in earnest*):

It's true.

PHIL:

You mean, like, you're happy.

TINY:

No, I mean, like, that guy is hot.

He points to a hot guy in a skintight yellow tank top—or some such article of clothing. You know, the kind where the guy looks more naked than if he were actually naked?

TINY:

And if I talked to him for a while and he had a good personality and respected me as a person I would let him kiss me on the mouth.

PHIL (*appearing not to comprehend*):

You're *gay*?

TINY:

Yeah. I know it's a shock. But I wanted you to be the first to know. Other than my parents, I mean.

As Phil continues to mime shock—strike up the band! The music begins.

["DUDE, YOU COULDN'T BE GAYER"]

PHIL (*singing now*):

You're gay?
Next you're gonna tell me the sky is blue,
that you use girl shampoo,
that critics don't appreciate Blink-182.
Oh, next you're gonna tell me the Pope is Catholic,

that hookers turn tricks,
that Elton John sucks HEY!

Tiny has shoved him playfully, and the song turns into a call-and-response. The choreography should have them dancing around the Pride parade, not unlike Ewan and Nicole dancing on top of the elephant in Moulin Rouge! *At some point, you might want to have the background Pridesters form a Rockettian kickline.*

TINY:

But I'm a football player!

PHIL:

Dude, you couldn't be gayer.

TINY:

I thought my straight-acting deserved Tonys.

PHIL:

You own a thousand My Little Ponies!

TINY:

Is it really so obvious?

PHIL:

Only in the same way that
the sun rises in the east,

The Lion King vilifies the wildebeest,
Harry Potter has a lightning scar,
and Republican politicians can be found sneaking into every gay bar.

TINY:

I'm gay!

PHIL:

Hey hey hey!

TINY:

Gayer than a three-dollar bill.

PHIL:

Gayer than *The Real Housewives of Beverly Hills*.

TINY:

Gayer than a Fire Island share.

PHIL:

Gayer than bleach-blond hair.

TINY:

I couldn't be gayer . . .

PHIL:

. . . if you memorized all seven seasons of *Buffy the Vampire Slayer*!

TINY:

I couldn't have a more homo strut . . .

PHIL:

. . . if Neil Patrick Harris was up your WHOA!

TINY:

And you don't mind?

PHIL:

No more than I mind
the sun setting in the west,
Dolly Parton's immortal chest,
puffy shirts at a Renaissance Fest,
or little birds chirping cutely in a nest.

You don't want me, do you?

TINY:

I would prefer a kangaroo!

PHIL:

Phew!

TINY:

True!

PHIL:

So can you abide
me showing some Tiny Cooper pride?

TINY:

No matter which direction I'm facin' . . .
I'm with Phil Wrayson!

Phil gives Tiny the straight-boy version of a hug, and Tiny engulfs him in response, as the Pridesters cheer and the number ends.

ACT I, SCENE 9

Tiny comes downstage again, as the Pride parade is turned into a locker room.

I will leave the stage directions of the following scene up to your discretion. I know certain members of certain musical societies who like to produce Damn Yankees *year after year just so they can have a gratuitous locker-room scene. You know, all the hot chorus members in towels and—whoops—maybe one of them falls a little. Especially if it's Broadway. There the towels fall a lot. Now, I am not suggesting you pander to the female and gay audience, even if those two demographics make up—what?—98 percent of all musical theatergoers? You decide what Lola wants in this case. And that's what she'll get.*

TINY:

Persuading Phil Wrayson and my parents to be on my side wasn't the biggest challenge. Nor were my friends anything less than accepting. There was only one group that I was really worried about—the football team.

It was freshman year, but I was already varsity, on account of my size. These guys barely knew me. And I didn't know how they'd feel about a gay boy in their midst.

I decided to confront them at the source of their fears: the locker room. It's something I don't get at all—almost every homophobic guy's worst-case scenario is being naked in a locker room with a gay guy. I mean, what's up with that? After I've just scrimmaged my ass off, the last thing I'm looking for is a quickie in the shower stall—with, incidentally, everyone else watching. I mean, come on. Get over your floppy self. If I'm going to ever fall for you, I'm going to do it the *right* way. I'll ask you out on a date, not run away with your towel.

Now, the trick was—how to get this across to them all? I wish I could say I thought it all out ahead of time . . . but I don't really plan my revelations. So it happened when I wasn't fully expecting it.

The guys—again, wearing whatever you want them to be wearing—have gathered in the locker room, doing locker room things. (Bully #1 and Bully #2 have returned from the baseball scene. I won't dignify them by giving them names.)

(Note: Phil Wrayson is NOT a member of the football team. We want this to be believable.)

Tiny comes walking into the scene, toweling his hair, singing:

TINY (*singing*):

I'm going to wash that boy right into my hair
I'm going to wash that boy right into my hair
I'm going to wash that boy right into my hair . . .

(*speaking*)

Oh, hi, guys.

There's silence for a moment. Then the bullies go into full attack mode.

["THE NOSE TACKLE (LIKES TIGHT ENDS)"]

BULLY #1:

The nose tackle likes tight ends!

BULLY #2:

Don't drop the soap, boys!
Don't drop the soap!

BULLY #1:

He'll penetrate your end zone unless you guard it!

BULLY #2:

Don't drop the soap, boys!
Don't drop the soap!

TINY:

Is that it?
Your biggest fear?
That all of a sudden
I'm after your rear?

The locker room isn't porn for me
because you're all so goddamn pimple-y.
I want touchdowns, man,
not to touch you there.
And if you have a problem with that
I can't say I care!

BULLY #1:

The nose tackle likes tight ends!

BULLY #2:

Don't drop the soap, boys!
Don't drop the soap!

BULLY #1:

He's aiming between your goalposts!

BULLY #2:

Don't drop the soap, boys!
Don't drop the soap!

TINY:

First of all, the soap is liquid,
so your warning makes no sense.

And for someone who's so straight and such
I think you doth protest too much.

You can keep in it your strap
'cause you ain't got nothing I want to tap.
I've come to win the game—
and hope you want the same.

BULLY #1:

The nose tackle likes tight ends!

TEAM (except for BULLIES):

Who cares, boys?
Who cares?

BULLY #2:

He wants you to go *long* and catch his pass!

TEAM (except for BULLIES):

Who cares, boys?
Who cares?

We joined this team so we could play,
not to hound you if you are gay.
Welcome, Tiny—ignore the haters.
They're just inexpert masturbators!

Our nose tackle likes tight ends!
If you attack him, we will defend!
Our nose tackle keeps his eyes on the balls!
Take him on, you take on us all!

Big dance number with the team protecting Tiny and ostracizing the bullies, perhaps with some towel action in homage to the towel number in the 2008 Lincoln Center revival of South Pacific.

At the end, Tiny looks relieved and grateful, proud to be gay and proud to be a part of this team.

TINY (*spoken*):

Thanks, guys.

The football players leave the stage, and Tiny revels in the security of being part of a team. As we head for the last scene in the first act, we feel he's in a pretty good place.

ACT I, SCENE 10

A dark stage. Tiny once more in the spotlight.

TINY:

So that was it. I had fully emerged from my big gay chrysalis and was now a big gay butterfly. I spread my wings. I flew around. It felt gooooood.

I had great friends. I had a supportive family. I had football. I should have felt complete.

And yet I didn't.

The piano begins. Tiny looks around the stage, as if he's just stepped outside the shtetl and is about to ask the immortal question, "Papa, can you hear me?" Only it's not his dead father he's addressing. For one, his father isn't dead. For two, that's already been done, like, a thousand times.

Tiny should remain in the spotlight throughout. The other characters should emerge from the darkness and then get spotlights of their own.

["WHAT IS MISSING? (LOVE IS MISSING)"]

TINY:

Something's missing.
What is missing?
It's like a sense I've never used.
A place I've never been.
A chord I've never heard.
A shiver I've never felt.

Lynda, the lesbian babysitter, emerges from the darkness.

LYNDA:

Something's missing?
What is missing?
It's a thought you've never mused.
A harmony in the din.
The height of the absurd.
A card you'll soon be dealt.

TINY:

Something's missing?
What is missing?

The Ghost of Oscar Wilde emerges and completes the trinity.

THE GHOST OF OSCAR WILDE:

It's the heart of the accused.
The fight you dare not win.
The sounds that make a word.
The unfastening of the belt.

TINY:

What is it?
What am I missing?
It's like a sense I've never used.

LYNDA:

It's a thought you've never mused.

THE GHOST OF OSCAR WILDE:

It's the heart of the accused.

TINY:

A place I've never been.

LYNDA:

A harmony in the din.

THE GHOST OF OSCAR WILDE:

The fight you dare not win.

TINY:

A chord I've never heard.

LYNDA:

The height of the absurd.

THE GHOST OF OSCAR WILDE:

The sounds that make a word.

TINY:

A shiver I've never felt.

LYNDA:

A card you'll soon be dealt.

THE GHOST OF OSCAR WILDE:

The unfastening of the belt.

LYNDA and THE GHOST OF OSCAR WILDE:

Something's missing.
What is missing?

TINY (*spoken*):

It's love, isn't it?

Lynda and The Ghost of Oscar Wilde nod, then resume singing.

LYNDA and THE GHOST OF OSCAR WILDE:

If act one in life is about finding yourself,
then act two is about finding everyone else.

TINY:

And love?

LYNDA and THE GHOST OF OSCAR WILDE:

And love.

THE GHOST OF OSCAR WILDE:

The pure and simple truth
is rarely pure and never simple.
What's a boy to do
when lies and truth are both considered
sinful?

Now it's Tiny's turn to nod.

TINY:

I was born this way,
and this is the way I've managed to stay.
Now I embark on the search for love.
Yes, now I embark on the search for love!

END OF ACT I

ACT II

ACT II, SCENE 1

Just in case you think, heading into Act II, that this is going to be one of those boy-meets-boy, boy-loses-boy, boy-gets-boy-back stories . . . the playwright must now point out the comedy of your error. Believe me, he had those notions at the start. He thought all he had to do was send love out into the universe and it would come back to him in the form of a perfect guy. A match. A soul mate. Remember the lesson Lynda gave him early on about halves? In the years since, he's forgotten it. It's not enough for him to be gay. He has to have a boyfriend. A you-are-my-everything boyfriend.

This is the dangerous thing about musicals. Most of them assume that as soon as you find your voice, you'll use it to sing to someone else. That way, you can get your enchanted evening, your seasons of love, your tale as old as time, your Camembert, your edelweiss.

The thing is, in musicals there's not a whole lot of looking (except in the case of Rodgers & Hammerstein's Cinderella.*) In musicals, things happen that throw you into love, whether it's gang warfare on the West Side, or a Nazi invasion, or needing a neighbor to light your candle.*

Real life doesn't provide quite so many openings. No, in real life, you've got to work a little harder to get to love.

I was willing to do the work. I was willing to look high and low for the perfect harmony.

I looked everywhere. *I dated a lot of boys.*

And what did I get out of it?

I got . . .

The Parade of Ex-boyfriends.

Yes, this second act has a pretty strange structure (although maybe not as strange as the second act of Follies, *right?). Here we're going to trace my progression as a person through my progression of breakups, because honestly at the time I couldn't tell the difference between the two. We're going to lose the Age button now and just go with the high school years as one entity. Because I'm sure that's going to be how they'll feel when they're over. Assuming they ever end.*

The next number calls for nineteen parts (including Tiny). I know that's a lot to ask of any production. So feel free to double- or triple-cast. Also feel free to give every ex a number somewhere on his costume, like this is the deli counter from dating hell. Whatever works. And, duh, the boyfriends can be played by girls dressed as boys. But you knew that already, I'm sure.

The key for the actor playing Tiny is to know this: I wanted it. I really, really wanted it. Keep that in mind at all times, even when I'm being foolish.

When the curtain rises, we see a swing set on the stage. There is a brief overture as Tiny swings on his own. Then the music stops for his opening monologue.

TINY:

Love is the most common miracle. Love is always a miracle, everywhere, every time. But for us, it's a little different. I don't want to say it's *more* miraculous—it is, though. Our miracle is different because some people say it's impossible. But let me tell you—it's possible. Very possible.

Tiny leaps off the swing and lands in what seems to be a heap.

TINY:

I fall and I fall and I fall and I fall and I fall. . . .

The swing set is wheeled off, and the **EX-BOYFRIENDS** *march onstage to the start of their song.*

["PARADE OF EX-BOYFRIENDS"]

CHORUS OF EX-BOYFRIENDS:

We are the parade of ex-boyfriends!

EX-BOYFRIEND #1:

You're too clingy.

EX-BOYFRIEND #2:

You're too sing-y.

EX-BOYFRIEND #3:

You're so massive.

EX-BOYFRIEND #4:

I'm just too passive.

EX-BOYFRIEND #5:

I'd rather be friends.

EX-BOYFRIEND #6:

I don't date tight ends.

EX-BOYFRIEND #7:

I found another guy.

EX-BOYFRIEND #8:

I don't have to tell you why.

EX-BOYFRIEND #9:

I don't feel the spark.

EX-BOYFRIEND #10:

It was only just a lark.

EX-BOYFRIEND #11:

You mean you won't put out?

EX-BOYFRIEND #12:

I can't conquer my doubt.

EX-BOYFRIEND #13:
I have other things to do.

EX-BOYFRIEND #14:
I have other guys to screw.

EX-BOYFRIEND #15:
Our love has all been in your head.

EX-BOYFRIEND #16:
I'm worried that you'll break my bed.

EX-BOYFRIEND #17:
I think I'll just stay home and read.

EX-BOYFRIEND #18:
I think you're in love with my need.

CHORUS OF EX-BOYFRIENDS:
Tiny Cooper, have no doubt:
You're the one we can live without.

TINY (*in a Sondheimian frenzy*):
What'd I do?
What'd I say?
Why did these boys
all go away?
I tried hard to be
who they'd want me to be
though most of the time

I couldn't help being me.
Was I too loud?
Too quiet?
Why work on the package
when there's no one to buy it?
Am I not enough of a gay?
Not enough of a guy?
My love life's a train wreck
so I might as well fly. . . .

CHORUS OF EX-BOYFRIENDS:

Parade!
Of the ex-boyfriends!
Any relationship that starts
inevitably ends!

EX-BOYFRIEND #1:

You wanted me too much.

EX-BOYFRIEND #2:

I can't be your emotional crutch.

EX-BOYFRIEND #3:

Just look at your size!

EX-BOYFRIEND #4:

You don't make my hormones rise.

EX-BOYFRIEND #5:

I'll see you around school.

EX-BOYFRIEND #6:
I hope that we're cool.

EX-BOYFRIEND #7:
I hope I'm not hurting you.

EX-BOYFRIEND #8:
I'm happily deserting you.

EX-BOYFRIEND #9:
You're drowning me in texts.

EX-BOYFRIEND #10:
I can't imagine us having sex.

EX-BOYFRIEND #11:
I guess I'm more of a slut.

EX-BOYFRIEND #12:
I need someone with a nicer butt.

EX-BOYFRIEND #13:
I never really thought it would work.

EX-BOYFRIEND #14:
Don't make it sound like *I'm* the jerk.

EX-BOYFRIEND #15:
You'll never, ever complete me.

EX-BOYFRIEND #16:

I don't mind if you want to delete me.

EX-BOYFRIEND #17:

I hate it when you hold my hand.

EX-BOYFRIEND #18:

I don't think you'll ever truly understand.

CHORUS and TINY:

The only way to learn
how to make something last
is to be yanked from your future
to reckon with the past.

Parade of ex-boyfriends
you thought you once knew.
Parade of ex-boyfriends,
who are all through with you.

CHORUS:

Your love life's a train wreck—

TINY:

—so I might as well fly.

CHORUS:

But you must hear our stories—

TINY:

—before I can try.

CHORUS:

Love is not easy.

TINY:

No matter how hard you pretend.

CHORUS:

Any relationship that starts—

TINY:

—inevitably ends.

CHORUS (*spoken*):

Except.

TINY:

Except?

CHORUS (*resumes singing*):

Except the one that transcends.

TINY:

Yes, the one that transcends.
Please send the one that transcends!

ACT II, SCENE 2

All the ex-boyfriends leave the stage. Ex-boyfriend #18, **WILL**, *might linger a little bit longer. Because, let's face it—he's the most recent, and those tend to linger longer. Which isn't to say I'm not over it. I am completely over it. Except for those moments when I'm not over it at all.*

But eventually Will leaves the stage. Because that's what he did—he left the stage. Took himself off. Exit, stage right. (Or stage left—whichever works for your blocking—I'm using this more as a metaphor than as a stage direction here.)

Tiny is now alone onstage. The parade has passed him by. But now it's going to return, slower this time, so he can see what's happened.

We are going back to the start of his dating life here—the first date.

As we approach the next song, he should look eager and excited. He's so naïve that he doesn't really feel too nervous—he actually thinks dating is going to be easy, now that he knows who he is. Try to capture that. Try to capture what it's like to have never squeezed yourself into the shape of someone else's expectations. Try to capture what it's like not to be thinking in terms of "types." Try to capture what's it like to have no exes, to have never failed. Try, if you can, to show that in the way Tiny is getting ready for tonight.

A mirror appears, and we see him comb his hair, maybe put on a kickass jacket. He's pulling out all the stops for this first date. Once he's judged himself lovable, he turns to the audience and begins his tale.

TINY:

My first date ever was with Brad Langley, who was a whole year older than me—which at the time meant *ninth grade*. Word of my outstanding outness had spread through the school like pink wildfire. Brad was bedazzled by the flames and traced them back to their source: yours truly.

BRAD *appears onstage. He is dressed with a kickassness similar to Tiny's.*

It really doesn't matter, but he is absolutely adorable.

BRAD (*a little shy*):

Hi. Are you Tiny?

TINY

(*not getting why this boy is approaching him*):

Do I *look* Tiny?

BRAD:

You look about as tiny as Idina Menzel's voice.

Now Brad has Tiny's attention.

TINY:

So *if* I tell you I appreciate that reference . . .

BRAD:

. . . *then* I'll know I'm talking to the right guy. Most people here don't know their Merman from their Martin.

TINY:

Heathens.

BRAD:

I *know*.

TINY (*to audience*):

Within minutes of our first conversation, we established all the things we had in common. And we kept having the same conversation for days, because we were enjoying it so much. If we started by talking about musicals, soon we were talking about *everything*.

The following is sung at first as a classic call-and-response—like "Anything You Can Do, I Can Do Better" only they're doing the opposite of disagreeing. This is about what it's like to find a kindred spirit, and what it's like to know you've found that kindred spirit by piecing together all the pop culture references you love. We need to see Tiny and Brad getting more and more excited as this part of the song plays out.

["I LIKE"]

TINY:

I like seeing Draco in Harry's arms.

BRAD (EX-BOYFRIEND #1):

I like succumbing to the Weasley boys' charms.

TINY:

I like singing in the shower.

BRAD:

I like singing at *any* hour.

TINY:

I like daydreaming about Cumberbatch.

BRAD:

I like keeping photos of him in my Sherlock stash.

TINY:

I like *Phantom of the Opera*—

BRAD:

—and the music of the night.

TINY:

I like "Bali Ha'i"—

BRAD:

—and when Emile sees the light.

TINY:

I like Idina in green—

BRAD:

And Judy on yellow.

TINY:

I like Patti at *don't cry*—

BRAD:

—and Barbra at *hello!*

TINY:

I like brown-paper packages—

BRAD:

—tied up in string!
I like the trolley bell—

TINY:

—that goes *ding ding ding!*

TINY and BRAD

(*spoken, completely bowled over by the serendipity of their synchronicity*):

Wow . . .

Tiny pauses to make an observation to the audience.

TINY:

Of course, once we saw we had all this in common, we got more personal. Because that's how it goes, right? You make enough mirror connections and you feel safe to fall below the surface, to get to the deeper truths you don't think are visible to the naked eye.

The song resumes.

TINY:

I like that my parents didn't kick me out of the
house.

BRAD:

I like that my stepfather isn't a louse.

TINY:

I like that I don't have to pretend.

BRAD:

I like that I don't think my life will end.

TINY:

I like that I don't have to worry about flirting.

BRAD:

I like that my soul is no longer hurting.

Tiny addresses the audience again. Brad remains paused in the conversation, oblivious.

TINY:

We kept talking and talking. And we didn't do anything else. I wanted to kiss him, to hold him, to be his boyfriend. But I had no idea what he wanted. This was the only thing we didn't talk about—the subject of us.

As we started a second month without clarifying the whole are-we-dating-and-are-we-going-to-kiss? thing, I found myself getting closer and closer to the edge of bringing it up.

The song resumes.

TINY:

I like to stare for hours at Cate Blanchett.

BRAD:

I like to watch as much Sandra Bullock as I
can get.

TINY:

I like to watch reruns of *Buffy* when I'm feeling huffy.

BRAD:

I like to turn on *Doctor Who* when I'm feeling blue.

TINY:

I like salted caramel ice cream.

BRAD:

I like Darren Criss and "Teenage Dream."

TINY:

I like Liza in Berlin—

BRAD:

—and Rita on the West Side.

TINY:

I like Nemo with his dad—

BRAD:

—and Simba with his pride.

TINY (*suddenly blurty*):

I like all of these things,
it's true.

But I also like
your body and
your smile,
your jacket
and your shoes,
your sweetness
and your jokes,
your style
and your smell.
In other words
what I guess I'm saying is
I like you.
Yes, you.
I really like you—
so much, too.
Yeah, it's true,
I really, really like you.
I mean,
I really, really, really like you.

BRAD (*spoken*):

Oh. Um . . . oh. Thanks?

TINY (*sung*):

I like you I like you I like you
I like you!
I like you!
I liiiiiiiiiiiiiiiii-ike you!

BRAD (*spoken*):

You really don't have to do that.

TINY (*getting really into it, not hearing Brad*):

I liiiii-ike you.
Oh yes.
Oh really.
I like you so so so so much.

BRAD (*spoken*):

We've only known each other a month.

TINY (*sung like "Tomorrow"*):

I like you,
I like you,
I may love you,
But now I like you . . .

BRAD:

I can't do this. I'm sorry, Tiny. But you've got to stop.

TINY (*sobering now, more plaintive*):

But I like you . . .
I really like you . . .

BRAD:

I'm going to go now.

TINY (*spoken now*):

But I like you.

BRAD:

I'm sorry. Really, I am. But I can't be that. I can't do that. I really have to go now.

Brad exits the stage.

TINY (*calling after him*):

I like you!

This last one is the one that's going to haunt him, the one that even he realizes is one too many, one too late. Brad isn't ready, and Tiny isn't ready for Brad not to be ready. So what might have been an amazing friendship gets dashed against the wall by romantic hopes. It's weird to look at now, to see that although I felt we were the same, we really weren't in the same place. I learned an important lesson: that just because a boy can recite the full tracklist to the [title of show] *cast album, it doesn't mean that he necessarily knows what the title of his own show is going to be.*

Of course, this lesson didn't come until much later. Right then, I didn't feel taught. I felt tricked and trapped and traumatized.

Which makes it time to send in the Friend Brigade.

Phil Wrayson enters from the side where Brad just left. Dialogue below is spoken, not sung.

PHIL:

It's okay. There are plenty of other boys out there. I'm sure you'll like one of them, too.

TINY:

But I like *him*.

PHIL:

I'm sure there's a better way to say this, but because that better way is just not occurring to me at the moment, I'm going to say it this way: He doesn't like you back. Not the way you want him to.

TINY:

But that's not fair!

PHIL:

I have absolutely no experience in this realm, but my gut instinct tells me that fairness isn't really what breaking up is about.

TINY:

Breaking up? Is that what just happened?

PHIL

(*looking to where Brad left, then turning again to Tiny*):

Unless he comes back here in the next five seconds, I would say so.

They both count out five seconds. Tiny uses his fingers. At five, he releases a big sigh.

TINY:

Does it get easier?

PHIL

(*looking and sounding like he has no idea what he's talking about*):

Sure! Of course!

Phil walks offstage. Which is really easy for him to do, considering.

TINY:

I thought I would be able to put Brad behind me and find someone better, smarter, more charming, and—most important—someone who liked me as much as I liked him. As the end of the school year came around, I dove right into the blue-eyed gaze of Silas, one of the other gay kids at our school. We didn't have much in common, but I thought that being gay in common would be enough. I overlooked the fact that when I started talking about *Les Misérables*, he asked me if it was in French. Or when I mentioned "Memory," he asked me what show it was from, and then found it *hysterical* that I would like a song that was sung by a cat. He'd talk to me, too, about things like politics, but I wasn't really listening. I was thinking of something else. Or, more accurately, some*one* else.

SILAS, *Ex-boyfriend #2, comes onstage and sits at a table—clearly, a date. Tiny sits at the table across from him. Looks him lovingly in the eye. The audience probably thinks, "Oh, this is going well." Then Tiny opens his mouth.*

TINY (*to the tune of "I LIKE"*):

Braaaaaaaaaaaad! Brad Brad Brad Brad Brad.
Brad Brad Brad.
Brad Brad.
Braaaaad.
Braaaaad!

Silas looks at him like he's crazy and leaves.

ACT II, SCENE 3

Lynda the babysitter enters, followed by The Ghost of Oscar Wilde.

TINY:

What are you doing here? Haven't you gone off to Oberlin by now? And who is that with you?

LYNDA:

This is more of a thematic interruption than a realistic one. And this is Oscar Wilde.

TINY:

What is Oscar Wilde doing here?

LYNDA:

He's proof that you can be a genius artist and still be a fool for love.

TINY:

I don't think I'm ready for that lesson yet.

Lynda dismisses The Ghost of Oscar Wilde from the stage. He goes without saying a word.

LYNDA:

You need to learn to put things in perspective.

TINY:

You say that, and all I hear is, "You need to stop being so crazy, Tiny Cooper."

LYNDA:

That's not what I said.

TINY:

But it's what I heard! And I'm *not* crazy. The issues with my ex-boyfriends aren't all my issues. They have issues, too.

LYNDA:

I know.

TINY (*as if she didn't just agree with him*):

Don't believe me? Send out exes #3, #12, and #16. They all broke up with me for basically the same reason.

LYNDA:

And what was that?

TINY:

My size.

EXES #3, #12, AND #16 *come out singing their lines from the parade. They seem disjointed out of the context of the song,* *like Cinderella and the others singing through the forest in the second act of* Into the Woods.

EX-BOYFRIEND #3:

You're so massive.

EX-BOYFRIEND #12:

I can't conquer my doubt.

EX-BOYFRIEND #16:

I'm worried that you'll break my bed.

EX-BOYFRIEND #3:

Just look at your size!

EX-BOYFRIEND #12:

I need someone with a nicer butt.

EX-BOYFRIEND #16:

I don't mind if you want to delete me.

The audience should feel uncomfortable here, because these are not comfortable things that the ex-boyfriends are saying.

Tiny stops addressing Lynda, who goes offstage as Tiny talks to the audience.

TINY:

You might ask: "Didn't they know what they were getting into from the start? It's not like you suddenly grew to be this size overnight!" To which I say: True. And I'm sure there were some people who were frightened away before they ever got to know me. Ex #3 was someone I met at the mall—we didn't really date. I just made sure to get invited to a party he was going to be at, and when I made my move, he called me massive and said, "Just look at your size," and that was the end of that. He counts as an ex because he made me feel dumped even without making me feel loved first.

Ex #12, Curtis, was different—I think he kept seeing me as his friends saw me, and wasn't strong enough to tell them to shut up. When it was just the two of us, when we could block out the world, it was fine. But no relationship should rely on you blocking out the world. The world will always get in. And if the world is going to make you self-conscious about dating a big-boned boy, that big-boned boy is going to notice.

As for Ex #16, Royce—he flirted with *everyone.* But if you ever liked him back, forget it. Some boys—not many, but a few—are like that, getting their own strength from finding your weakness and poking it. There's something weirdly transfixing about their confidence, like even as they're condescending to you, you're secretly hoping that their strength will rub off and suddenly you'll be as confident as they are. But that's not how it works. Being strong at being a jerk isn't really strength—it's just being a jerk. It may make these guys great Future Business Leaders of America, but it makes them really crappy boyfriends.

Now, about the number that's going to soon unfold. Even though there are plenty of people like me who worship at its altar, musical theater is not particularly kind to its larger-of-frame characters. In opera, we get arias, romance, intrigue. In musical theater, we're comic relief (when we're allowed to be there at all). When the fat boy dances, it's usually to get a laugh. But not here. Not in my *show.*

Here is what I want you to do. This is really two songs in one . . . but the audience won't know that at first. For the first part, make it as campy as you want. Let them see the fat boy dance! But when the second part starts, strip that all away. Make it sincere. Think about what they were able to do in Kinky Boots. *At first it's all "hey, drag queens, ha ha ha"—but then at the end Billy Porter gets his big number and he sells it like he's getting a commission. There's no ha ha ha. There's just a beautiful woman rising above her pain and all the shit she's been given her whole life. What I'm writing here isn't as good, but try to give it that power.*

It's exactly what Ex-boyfriends #3, #12, and #16 would not want you to do. Imagine them sitting in the audience as you're singing this. Imagine them laughing at you at the start. And then try to imagine them realizing they were wrong about you.

At first, Tiny looks wounded. But then he stares them down as the music starts to swell. He'll be singing this one to them, until the chorus comes in. Then he'll be playing to the audience, until the final turn.

["THE SIZE OF THE PACKAGE"]

TINY:

What, you think you know me?
Nothing funnier than the fat boy.
What, you think you got this?
Who am I to even think of love?

This part's the disco windup. The Jennifer Holliday/Hudson swell. The chorus comes onto the stage to back Tiny up.

Well, your love's the empty calorie here.
You say I'm so huge but you don't see me at all.
So wipe those smirks from each one of your
faces—
'cause I know I'm big-boned and beautiful in
all the right places.

TINY and CHORUS (*in full disco tilt*):

It's not the size of the package,
it's the size of the soul.
It's not the body you have,
it's the life as a whole.

It's not the size of the package,
the moves make the man.
It's not the weight of the words,
it's that you say what you can.

TINY:

I was once a little boy—
oh no, I was never a little boy!
I have always lived large
and in charge.
And if you can't carry that
I'm going to drop right out of your life!

TINY and CHORUS:

It's not the size of the package,
it's the size of the thrill.
It's not the tip of the scale,
it's the lift of the will.

It's not the size of the package
that's the source of your pride.
It's not the stretch of the belly,
it's the fire inside.

TINY:

I was once a little boy—
oh no, I was never a little boy!
I have always lived large
and in charge.
And if you can't carry that
I'm going to drop right out of your life!

A fun dance interlude follows—fat boy dancing ha ha ha—although please be sure Tiny maintains his dignity throughout. As it's happening, he realizes the exes are watching. And as much as he wants to win them over . . . he's not winning them over. The last refrain is less assured than before. The chorus, fading into the background, keeps looking at the exes.

TINY and CHORUS:

It's not the size of the package,
it's the size of the heart.
It's not the body you see—

Tiny stops at the third line, looking at the exes. #3 and #16 are laughing at him. #12 looks embarrassed to have seen what he's just seen.

TINY

(*plaintive now, to the exes, the tempo slowed considerably*):

What, you think you know me?
Nothing funnier than the fat boy.
What, you think you got this?
Who am I to even think of love?

That last line should linger through the theater. People should understand what the exes' laughter means to Tiny. Even if he's proud, he's not invulnerable to doubt. If you think one musical number gets rid of all his insecurities, think again. He knows what's right and what's wrong. But he doesn't feel it yet. And while it's great to know the right words, in order for them to become your truth, you have to feel them, too.

Fade to black.

ACT II, SCENE 4

While Tiny changes costumes very quickly, Phil Wrayson comes onto the stage.

PHIL WRAYSON:

I am not proud of the fact that Tiny's fourth ex-boyfriend was my fault. And I would like to publicly apologize to Tiny for everything that happened.

TINY (*offstage*):

Apology accepted!

PHIL WRAYSON:

It was my cousin. Well, not really my cousin. But my mother's sister's best friend from college's son who was in town for three days. So, cousin-ish. Maybe not even first cousin-ish. Second cousin-ish. Like, if I were King of Illinois and I died, this guy would be something like three hundred ninety-fifth in line for the throne.

TINY (*offstage*):

You've made your point! Now get to the good part!

PHIL WRAYSON:

The good part is that for two of the three days he was here, this guy dated Tiny Cooper.

TINY (*offstage*):

Now get to the bad part!

PHIL WRAYSON:

The bad part is that this guy only dated Tiny Cooper because he was bored out of his skull staying with us, and when he was given the choice of going out on two dates with Tiny Cooper or staying in and playing Scrabble with me and my parents, he chose to go on the dates with Tiny Cooper. Tiny did not know this at the time.

TINY (*offstage*):

I thought it was love!

PHIL WRAYSON:

He thought it was love. When, in fact, it was like three hundred ninety-fifth in line for love. When it was time for this guy to go, he didn't even ask for Tiny's e-mail address or phone number or mailing address. In the intervening year and a half, we've all forgotten his name.

TINY (*offstage*):

It was Octavio!

PHIL WRAYSON (*to audience*):

It was not Octavio.

TINY (*offstage*):

It's Octavio if I want it to be!

PHIL WRAYSON (*to Tiny offstage*):

Is that even a name?!?

TINY (*offstage*):

. . . (*stubborn silence*)

PHIL WRAYSON (*to audience*):

For the purpose of this play, he shall be known as Octavio. Octavio, please come out here and take a bow. Let's hear it for Octavio!

Phil Wrayson starts clapping. This hopefully leads the audience to start clapping. It becomes a little awkward. Ex-boyfriend #4 does not show up.

TINY (*offstage*):

He's already left!

PHIL WRAYSON:

This seems somehow fitting. Shall we move on to Ex-boyfriend #5?

Ex-boyfriend #5 appears onstage. Like many of the boys Tiny's attracted to, he's an actor. (If that last sentence raised a big red flag for you, that means you've tried to date an actor.) Now, it could certainly be said that I've spent a good portion of my days going through life like it's my own musical. But I think that's okay, since it's my own musical. **JIMMY**, *on the other hand, tended to think he was at the center of his own Shakespearean play. He was pompous and pretentious and I still would have iambed his pentameter for five acts or more if he'd let me.*

By dating actors, you think they'll let you in on the act. Most of the time, though, there's only five stages of grief to be found.

But not yet! This is a sweet scene. Because it really was a sweet thing, while it lasted.

Three chairs are moved onto the stage, to simulate movie theater seats.

PHIL WRAYSON:

I'll see you all later.

Tiny comes bounding onstage in a new outfit, holding a movie theater bucket of popcorn.

JIMMY (EX-BOYFRIEND #5):

Tiny! Over here!

TINY (*clearly excited about a date*):

Hey!

JIMMY:

I hope these seats are good?

TINY:

Whenever I have a dream that takes place in a movie theater, if it's a good dream, I am sitting in these exact seats.

They move to sit down, Tiny first. As he's sitting down in his seat, he puts the bucket of popcorn on the seat next to him. Jimmy, thinking this means Tiny is going to keep it there, sits down in the seat next to it. Tiny realizes this too late, and keeps the bucket in between them.

JIMMY:

I'm so glad it's summer. And I'm so glad we have a chance to hang out!

TINY:

Yeah! I mean, I went and saw you in *Othello* three times, and not once did I realize that you were—

JIMMY:

Queer as a flamingo in drag?

TINY:

Now, *that's* acting.

We hear the start of a movie projector. They both go for popcorn at the same time. Their hands touch. There's a brief charge, but then Jimmy pulls away.

JIMMY:

After you.

TINY:

No, after you.

JIMMY:

I insist.

Tiny takes a massive handful of popcorn. Then he realizes there's no classy way of eating this. After Jimmy takes a more manageable portion, Tiny puts some back, to make his manageable, too.

This sets the tone for the number, which will be sung by a **MOVIE STAR** *on the corner of the stage, in a spotlight and with a backdrop that should look like a movie screen. (Maybe, to make it clear, start by projecting the 9-8-7 test pattern on her like at the start of an old movie.) (Or him—the movie star can be whoever you want. For the movie, I'd like Anne Hathaway, but like in the* Twelfth Night *she did at Shakespeare in the Park, not her my-bad-haircut-killed-me performance in the* Les Miz *movie.)*

As the movie star is singing, there should be elaborate romantic choreography between Jimmy and Tiny. At first, just flirtation over the popcorn. Some "accidental" hand touching. Some popcorn sharing—trying to throw it in each other's mouth, etc. Some leaning. Finally, Jimmy moves the popcorn and takes the second seat. A kiss gets closer. At one point, Tiny goes in for it, but Jimmy's just taken a mouthful of popcorn. It should be funny and sweet. The audience should forget that Jimmy is an ex. The audience should think there's potential here. Because, of course, at the time Tiny wasn't seeing Jimmy as a future ex. He was seeing Jimmy as a future.

["CLOSE TO A KISS"]

MOVIE STAR:

The stage is set—
The lights are dim—
Just a gasp of distance
between you and him—

The last low word
has left your lips—
so it's time to use them
to get your bliss . . .

Is there anything
better than this?
When you are close
so close
to a kiss?

One thought—
two minds
Two hearts—
one time . . .

The stage is set—
The lights are dim—
Just a gasp of distance
between you and him—

The last low word
has left your lips—
so it's time to use them
to get your bliss . . .

Is there anything
better than this?
When you are close
so close
to a kiss?

Don't take your time—
take his!
Because you are close
so close
to a kiss . . .

They kiss. It is Tiny's first kiss. And Jimmy's third.
It's magical.
They pull apart. Then kiss again. And again.

The emotions rise in Tiny. He has to sing it.

TINY:

I like you!
Yes, you.
I really like you!
So much, too!
Yeah, it's true—
I really, really like you.
I mean,
Really, really, really like you!

JIMMY (*spoken*):
I like you, too. And time goes by.

TINY:
I like you I like you I like you
I like you!
I like you!
I liiiiiiiiiiiiiiiiii-ike you!

JIMMY (*spoken*):
I like you, too. But maybe just maybe . . .

TINY

(*getting really into it, not really hearing Jimmy*):

I liiiii-ike you.
Oh yes.
Oh really.
I like you so so so so much.

JIMMY (*spoken*):

I like you, Tiny. But I'm not sure I like you in that way.

TINY (*spoken*):

What?

We lead directly into the next number . . .

["YOU'RE WONDERFUL! I DON'T WANT TO DATE YOU!"]

JIMMY:

You're wonderful!
I don't want to date you!
You're amazing!
I would much rather be your friend!

You're special!
So why ruin it?
You're fantastic!
I'm not really sure you're my type!

TINY (*spoken*):

What? Fantastic isn't your type?

JIMMY:

You're stupendous!
But I can't take you seriously!
You're incredible!
And it was bound to end eventually!

You're the best!
And I don't want to hurt you!
You're remarkable!
But I can't stay with you just because you want
me to!

TINY (*spoken*):

This means no more kissing, right?

Jimmy leans in to kiss Tiny. But this time it's on the cheek.

JIMMY:

You're marvelous!
I don't expect you'll understand!
You're delectable!
I know you'll find another man!
And that other man can be
as wonderful to you
as you are to me!
Only he'll feel the same
and it won't be as lame
as me saying:

You're wonderful!
But I can't date you!

Jimmy exits.

TINY:

But I don't want anyone else! (*to audience*) Or at least I thought I didn't want anyone else. Then a few days passed. The Jimmy-sized hole in my life got smaller and smaller until I didn't even feel it anymore.

I swore I would never date an actor again. Then I realized, um, I *am* an actor, so I had to hope that some other guy out there wasn't swearing *he'd* never date an actor.

Mostly, I felt I had to widen the dating pool, because right now it was feeling pretty kiddie-sized. And even if I wasn't quite ready to dive into the ocean of guys that was waiting for me after high school, I could at least find something of Olympic proportions.

Which is why I asked my parents to send me to drama camp.

I wanted my spring awakening, even if it was

coming a season late. I wanted summer lovin' that would happen so fast. I wanted to succeed at the business of love without really trying.

My mother sewed my name into all my underwear. But, really, it was another boy's name I was ready to sew into my heart.

(*looks down at clothes*) I can't possibly wear this to Camp Starstruck. I'll be right back.

Tiny leaves the stage and changes into summer garb as Camp Starstruck is assembled on the stage in some manner by a variety of extremely enthusiastic musical-theater campers.

ACT II, SCENE 5

Tiny strides out in summer wear. When Joseph Templeton Oglethorpe the Third is mentioned, Ex-boyfriend #6 appears—he should be dressed as some character from some play. Use whatever garb is available, although Shakespearean dress would be pretty funny—this is yet another actor for Tiny to date.

The chorus should be Tiny's fellow campers, each one more of a drama queen than the last. 'Cause that's the way it is. (For further reference, please read E. Lockhart's definitive tome on the subject, Dramarama.*) Joseph sings along with the chorus, except for the chorus's last line.*

TINY:

(*looking down at clothes*) Much better, right?

Welcome to Camp Starstruck. Land of the misfit boys, and all the girls who love them. We put on eight musicals in eight weeks—one minute you'd be bloody, bloody Andrew Jackson, and then you'd blink and you'd be Daddy Warbucks or Porgy or Bess. The directors had all the power, and we worshipped and reviled them accordingly. The food wasn't up to *Oliver!*'s standards, the heat was somewhere between *Oklahoma!* and *110 in the Shade*, and the mattresses were more pea than princess.

But none of that really mattered. I had found my tribe. It felt like a family reunion for the family I'd never really known, a homecoming at the place where I was always meant to be but hadn't known how to find.

The other campers have now finished setting up the camp, and Tiny's ready to sing.

["SUMMER OF GAY"]

TINY:

There was a time
when I thought I liked vagina—
but then came a summer
when I realized something finer . . .

JOSEPH *appears.*

I knew from the moment he took top bunk
how desperately I wanted into his trunk.
Joseph Templeton Oglethorpe the Third
left my heart singing like a little bird.

TINY and CHORUS:

Summer of gay!

So lovely! So queer!
Summer of gay—

TINY:

—set the tone for my year!

Mama and Papa didn't know
they were lighting the lamp
the moment they sent me to
Starstruck Drama Camp.

So many Hamlets to choose from—
some tortured, some cute.
I was all ready to sword-fight
or take the Ophelia route.

There were boys who called me sister
and sistahs who taught me about boys.
Joseph whispered me sweet nothings—

Joseph whispers him sweet nothings.

—and I fed him Almond Joys.

Tiny feeds him Almond Joys.

TINY and CHORUS:

Summer of gay!
So fruity! So whole!
Summer of gay—

TINY:

—I realized Angel would be my role!

Mama and Papa didn't know
how well their money was spent
when I learned about love
from our production of *Rent.*

Tiny wraps his arms around Joseph.

Such kissing on the catwalks!
Such competition for the leads!
We fell in love so often and fully—

CHORUS:

—across all races and sexualities and creeds!

TINY and CHORUS:

Summer of gay!
Ended soon! Lasted long!
Summer of gay—

TINY:

—my heart still carries its song!

Joseph leaves Tiny's embrace, goes offstage. The tempo slows, in an "It turned colder" sort of way.

Joseph and I didn't make it to September . . .
but you can't unlight a gay-colored ember.
I will never go back
to the heterosexual way
'cause now every day—

CHORUS:

—yes, every day—

TINY:

—is the sum-mer
of gay!

Fade to black. Or whatever color you like. If you can find a way to fade to pink or purple, please do.

ACT II, SCENE 6

When Tiny returns to the stage, he's back in school clothes. Summer at Starstruck has given him what he needs—a sense that there's somewhere he really, really belongs.

Now, don't get me wrong—as you can see in the first act, my family was actually pretty cool about me being me. That's important. But I wasn't about to hang out with my parents for the rest of my life. I had to start making that second family, the one you choose once you're given a choice. Starstruck made me see what that was like, on a limited-time basis. Now I had to start doing that at home.

TINY (*spoken*):

I came back to school ready to be the big gay star I was meant to be. The breakup with Joseph was the first one that made sense. We could have tried long distance, but I didn't like long distance—I didn't see the point of having a boyfriend if I couldn't have him next to me. Joseph and I cried our summertime tears, for sure. But the thing about summertime tears is that you know they're made out of summertime. They evaporate when the school year begins. Joseph and I had an honest discussion about this as we said good-bye. I thought, hey, this must mean I'm growing up.

And I wasn't the only one who'd grown up.

I returned to my high school to find that the rainbow had connected, big-time. I used to be able to count the number of gay kids on one jazz hand, but now there seemed to be more gay kids in our high school than there were minutes in *Miss Saigon*. I plunged right in.

EX-BOYFRIEND #7 *enters. He looks like a lost puppy, but has the heart of a bitch.*

TINY:

Evan was new to town. I showed him around. The tour included my bedroom.

Within two weeks, he wanted off my welcome wagon.

EX-BOYFRIEND #7 (*reprise from "Parade"*):

I've found another guy!

TINY (*spoken*):

He felt bad about it, but he had a crush on someone else. I'm sure I would've dwelt on it . . . but three days later, I found myself flirting for the first time during football practice. His name was Ramon. He'd been on my team since fifth grade.

EX-BOYFRIEND #8 *enters and stands next to Ex-boyfriend #7. Bonus points if Ex-boyfriend #8 played a non-bully football team member from earlier.*

TINY:

I thought we had so so so much in common. But he fumbled all of my passes, and soon I sensed his heart wasn't in the game. It only took nine days for him to tell me he wanted to bring our relationship off the field. I begged him for an explanation.

EX-BOYFRIEND #8 (*reprise from "Parade"*):

I don't have to tell you why!

. . . but as he sings the line, he takes Ex-boyfriend #7's hand. They look each other lovingly.

TINY:

Evan and Ramon started dating the next week.

EX-BOYFRIEND #7 (*sung*):

I like you!

EX-BOYFRIEND #8:

I like you!

EX-BOYFRIENDS #7 and #8 TOGETHER:

I like you so, so much!

They skip off the stage together. As they do, they pass Phil, who's walking in.

PHIL:

Hey.

TINY:

Hey.

PHIL:

I heard about Ramon. And Evan. And I think you were maybe dating one of them? Or even both of them? Either way, that sucks.

TINY (*coming slightly unhinged*):

I don't understand! What is the point of being the big gay star I was meant to be if nobody wants to date me past the first trimester? It's like a cruel joke—to work so hard to be completely me, and then to feel so incomplete.

PHIL:

You don't need to have a boyfriend to be complete. For example, I don't have a girlfriend. And look at me.

TINY:

I *know*. Look at you!

Tiny gives Phil the once-over. It's clear that he's concerned.

PHIL:

If attacking me makes you feel better, I will allow you to do so for two more minutes. But only because you've just had either one or two boys break up with you.

TINY (*shaking his head*):

No. It's not you I should be attacking. Clearly, it's me.

PHIL:

That's not what I meant.

TINY:

I'm repulsive!

PHIL:

You're hardly repulsive.

TINY:

But I repel people!

PHIL:

Please tell me this pity party ends early. Or at least serves cake.

TINY:

I'm unlovable!

PHIL:

Your mommy and daddy and fwiends wuv you very much.

TINY:

But most of all, worst of all, I'm inadequate!

PHIL:

Inadequate.

TINY:

Inadequate! A boy may look my way, but he never stays longer than a few days. How is that supposed to make me feel?

PHIL:

But, Tiny—

TINY:

No, Phil. For just one moment, I want you to act like a girl. Be my friend, but be my friend like a girl would be my friend, not like a straight boy would be my friend. That's the only way you're going to understand.

I know I shouldn't want it so much. I know I should be happy alone. But all I can feel is the missing piece. All I can feel is—inadequate! A boy may say he's mine, but after a very short time, he forgets why.

PHIL:

Don't be so hard on yourself!

TINY:

Sweet of you to say! But you know what? No matter how much I love myself, I'll wonder why no one else will love me. No matter how loud I sing, I'll wonder why there isn't another voice there, singing right back.

PHIL:

I'm here.

TINY:

Yeah, well, you don't count.

PHIL:

It's not all about romance, Tiny. There are other kinds of love.

TINY (*covering ears*):

I CAN'T HEAR YOU.

Ex-boyfriend #9 comes sauntering across the stage. **DEVON CHANG**. *Oh, man, Devon Chang. Sometime over the summer, he went from geek to god, and became The Boy Who Launched a Thousand Texts.*

Tiny is distracted from Phil as he and Devon make eye contact. There is some wordless flirtation. Devon starts to walk off the stage.

TINY (to PHIL):

I'll be right back.

Tiny runs after Ex-boyfriend #9, leaving Phil alone onstage. (Don't judge. Real friends understand.)

ACT II, SCENE 7

PHIL

(*looking offstage, then turning to the audience*):
We can only wish them the best. Let's see how it went.

At this point, **DJANE** *comes out. (In a former incarnation of this musical, she was Janey, but I think Djane fits her personality better.) I hope Phil and Djane don't mind me saying this in the stage directions, but Djane is the girl that Phil Wrayson should really be going out with. It would have happened long ago, if they didn't keep getting in its way.*

Djane shakes her head.

PHIL:

No luck?

DJANE:

All of the clovers had three leaves.

PHIL (*thinks for a second*):

Oh, I see what you did there.

DJANE:

All he found at the end of the rainbow was a pot of—

PHIL:

Stop! This is a family show.

DJANE (*deadpan*):

In what way is this a family show?

Phil just looks at her.

DJANE:

What?

PHIL:

It's just that . . . I don't know . . . you look nice?

Djane gazes at him strangely.

DJANE:

Now, why would you do that?

PHIL:

Because you look nice-ish?

DJANE:

Oh, now it's nice-ish.

PHIL:

My head is starting to hurt from contemplating all the possible ways I could offend you.

DJANE:

Why would you choose now, of all times, to tell me I look nice-ish?

TINY (*offstage*):

I'm ready for the next number!

DJANE:

I've got to go make sure Oscar Wilde knows his lines.

Djane exits.

PHIL (*flustered, calling after her*):

Now, don't get too Wilde now, you hear? That man could win an *Oscar* for his *Wilde*-ness! (*to audience*) Lord, did I just say that? I guess it all goes to show—I'm making a transition here—that love sometimes causes you to do stupid things. And even when the lessons are clear to everyone else around you, sometimes you have a hard time seeing them yourself. When people say love is blind, they act like that's a good thing. But some people find their way around in the darkness a little better than others.

Tiny is wheeled onto stage in a bed (if a rolling bed is readily available). He is wearing a pair of silk pajamas. At first it looks like he is asleep. But then he is illuminated by a cell-phone glow, and it's clear that he's texting.

PHIL:

Even if someone told Tiny it was over, he wanted to believe it wasn't. Perhaps because it was easy to see him coming, he didn't make it a habit of chasing people down IRL. But a phone—a phone couldn't run away. It would just keep receiving text after text after text. So he kept sending text after text after text.

As Tiny falls asleep, Ex-boyfriends #9, 13, 15, and 17 appear on the side of the stage and sing the following in a round, to the tune of "Row Row Row Your Boat." #9 sings a full verse first, then repeats, and the others chime in, in a round.

EX-BOYFRIEND #9:

Text text text your heart all across the screen,
scarily scarily scarily scarily, love's not meant to be.

Text text text your heart all across the screen,
scarily scarily scarily scarily, love's not meant to be.

EX-BOYFRIEND #13:

Text text text your heart all across the screen,
scarily scarily scarily scarily, love's not meant to be.

EX-BOYFRIEND #15:

Text text text your heart all across the screen,
scarily scarily scarily scarily, love's not meant to be.

EX-BOYFRIEND #17:

Text text text your heart all across the screen,
scarily scarily scarily scarily, love's not meant to be.

TINY wakes with a start as soon as they're done. Phil Wrayson has left the stage. In his place is The Ghost of Oscar Wilde. (Bonus points if you can make his appearance a surprise.)

TINY:

Who are you?

THE GHOST OF OSCAR WILDE:

Why, I'm the ghost of Oscar Wilde, making a visitation to you while you sleep.

TINY:

Because of my singular promise as a dramatist?

THE GHOST OF OSCAR WILDE:

More because of your disappointing love life and

the behavior that results from it. I have seen your manic LOLs, and I'm not laughing. No. This is an intervention. Put the phone down.

Tiny will not relinquish the phone. He surreptitiously tries to finish a text.

THE GHOST OF OSCAR WILDE (*unaccountably shrill*):
STEP AWAY FROM THE PHONE! PUT YOUR HANDS UP AND STEP AWAY FROM THE PHONE!

Tiny, not ready for such shrillness, especially from an Irish theatrical legend, drops his phone onto the bed. The Ghost of Oscar Wilde picks it up and powers it off.

THE GHOST OF OSCAR WILDE (*back to politeness*):
Good. Now please, allow me to share some hard-won wisdom, from one green-carnation wearer to another.

Music begins.

["DON'T HIT SEND"]

THE GHOST OF OSCAR WILDE:

Take some advice from me
as I wander around eternally
thinking of the love I lost
and all the things it cost.
I fell for Bosie's bottomy guile
and lost my wings in a sodomy trial.
Surrounded in jail by thieves and rakes,
I had plenty of time to ponder my mistakes.

I can't say I regret breaking nature's laws
but I do regret not taking a pause
to see there was far from a surfeit
of evidence saying the boy was worth it.

Believe me, I understand the urge
to push all your means to an end.
But I must intercede here and inform you now:
Whatever you do, do not hit send!

You think it's a good idea—
but it's not.
You think you have something new to say—
but you don't.
It's common enough behavior
to think that words can be your savior
but they cannot raise the dead
or change the thoughts inside his head.

When you text the seventh time
with no word from the other side
it's a sign, my friend
and the sign says END.

It used to be
if you wanted to embarrass yourself
you'd have to wait a few days
for the embarrassment to be delivered.
But now in an instant
of desire most insistent
you cross before you've looked
and your rawness leaves you cooked.

Don't hit send!
Don't think for a second
that your phone is your friend.
You may be afraid of pauses
but every pause has its causes!

You think it's a good idea—
but it's not.
You think you have something new to say—
but you don't.
It's common enough behavior
to think that words can be your savior
but they cannot raise the dead
or change the thoughts inside his head.
When you text the seventh time
with no word from the other side

it's a sign, my friend,
and the sign says END.

It used to be
if you wanted to embarrass yourself
you'd have to wait a few days
for the embarrassment to be delivered.
But now in an instant
of desire most insistent
you've managed to destroy
any last chance you had with the boy!

Don't hit send!
Don't think for a second
that your phone is your friend.
You may be afraid of pauses
but every pause has its causes.
More words will not persuade him—
they'll only infuriate him.
So take if from me
whatever you do—
Do not . . . hit . . . send!

On that note, The Ghost of Oscar Wilde finishes his song, hopefully to more applause than he got toward the end of his life.

OSCAR (to TINY):

Believe me, I understand all the modern dickstractions—I mean, *dis*tractions—that you have. Especially on your phones. I admire your feverish belief in the power of words to keep a connection going even when it's not there. But you only have so many words in your life, Tiny, and rather than giving them all away, you should keep some for yourself.

TINY:

What do you mean?

OSCAR (*reciting, not singing*):

Look forward to the moment
when it all falls apart.
Look forward to the moment
when you must rearrange your heart.

It might feel like the end of the world—
but it's the beginning of your art.

TINY:

Texting? That's my art?

OSCAR (*shaking his head*):

No, Tiny. Words. *Passion.* The danger of falling in love is that you mistakenly believe the loved one is the only source of passion in your life. But there is passion everywhere. In music. In words. In the stories you tell and the stories you see. Find your passion everywhere, and share it widely. Don't narrow it down to one thin line.

TINY:

But you don't choose to fall in love, do you? Don't you just fall?

OSCAR:

You fall and you fall and you fall. There are things you cannot control. But that is why you must hold on to the things you *can* control.

I will let you in on a secret, Tiny. Are you ready?

TINY:

Yes.

OSCAR (*on the verge of disappearing*):

You think you're an actor, Tiny. We all think we are actors, given our scripts. But really? You're the playwright. You're the composer.

Before Tiny can ask any more questions, The Ghost of Oscar Wilde has vanished just as strangely as he appeared.

ACT II, SCENE 8

Tiny remains in bed.

TINY:

It was, to say the least, a strange visitation—and I didn't know what it meant. Not yet.

As if I wasn't confused enough, as high school continued and my high school relationships continued, I found the whole sex question kept coming up. The question being: Are we going to do it or what?

Now, don't get me wrong. I think making out is awesome. And I knew that when I was ready, sex would be awesome, too.

But I wasn't ready. And some of the guys I was dating were more than ready.

EX-BOYFRIENDS #10, #11, AND #14 *come onstage and circle the bed.*

EX-BOYFRIENDS #10/#11/#14:

Horny horny horny—
we're just so
horny horny horny.

TINY (*looking at them with dismay*):
The pressure was intense. And it made me realize that although I had all of these gay exes in my life, I didn't really have a gay friend. So I called Djane instead.

Djane appears on the corner of the stage, holding her phone to her ear. Tiny uses the phone he was using to text in bed.

TINY (to DJANE):
I know I'm a guy, so I should not make such rash generalizations—but, wow, guys can really get stuck on sex.

EX-BOYFRIENDS #10/#11/#14 (*murmuring as he talks*):
Horny horny horny—
we're just so
horny horny horny.

Horny horny horny—
we're just so
horny horny

TINY:
(*To Exes*) Stop that! (*To Djane*) You see?

DJANE:
Can I give you some advice that sounds massively

oversimplistic but is actually, I've found, somewhat helpful?

TINY:

Sure.

DJANE:

Ninety-seven percent of the time, it all comes down this: *Don't do what you don't want to do.* Ask yourself that simple question: *Do I want to do this?* If the answer is yes, go for it. If it's anything but yes, don't.

EX-BOYFRIENDS #10/#11/#14

(*singing one verse, then singing softly under the following dialogue*):

Horny horny horny.
Horny horny horny.

DJANE:

Do any of them appeal to you?

TINY:

Not like this.

DJANE:

Do they care about you the way they should?

TINY:

No.

DJANE:

Do you want to do it?

TINY:

No.

DJANE:

There you go.

TINY:

But how do I tell them?

DJANE:

You're Tiny Cooper. You mop them up with a song.

Tiny understands. As the song begins with some serious chordage, he gets out of bed and is joined by three backup dancers wearing matching pajamas. They are the ones who will mop up the ex-boyfriends while Tiny sings.

["SAVING MYSELF"]

TINY:

All you boys who just want to mess around!
All you boys who can't put up with me not
putting out!
I've got something to say to you—
and it goes something like this.

I'm saving myself for someone who treats me
better!
I'm saving myself for one I won't regret!
If you want to go all the way,
I have to know you're gonna stay
'cause I'm saving myself for someone
who treats me better.

As Tiny sings the following, the backup dancers school the exes.

Keep it in your pants
and ask me to dance!

Get away from the bed
and talk to me instead!

We're not going to go there
until you handle me with care!

EX-BOYFRIENDS #10/#11/#14
(*trying to fight back against the dancers*):
Horny horny horny!
We're just so
horny horny horny!

TINY

(*as the dancers put the exes in their place*):

If you're just doing it 'cause you're horny,
my bush is gonna be thorny!
I'm telling you—
I'm saving myself for someone who treats me
better!
I'm saving myself for one I won't regret!
If you want to go all the way,
I have to know you're gonna stay
'cause I'm saving myself for someone
who treats me better.

If you want to go all the way
you better give me the time of day—
when other people see us together—
when other people are around.

I'm not a game that you're playing.
I'm not a lie that you're saying.
I am worth so much more than that.
Yes, I am worth so much more than that.

Someday my prince will come,
and when he does,
we'll come and come and *come*.
But 'til that day I'm saving myself.
Oh, yes, I'm saving myself from you.

Because I am worth so much more than that.
Yes, I am worth so much more than that!

The number ends with Tiny slipping off to change while the backup dancers triumph once and for all over the exes, ultimately knocking all three of them into the bed and wheeling them offstage.

ACT II, SCENE 9

Tiny emerges wearing something casual—a T-shirt and jeans, perhaps. Whatever's handy. It's one of his less dynamic outfits.

TINY:

That felt good. For a day or two. Then I was back to trying. And failing.

Ex-boyfriends #13 through #17 come onto the stage and walk in a ring around Tiny.

TINY:

I exhausted them. They exhausted me. They lied about their hair color. I lied about liking their hair color. I swooned—and then I realized that swooning is really just another way of saying *losing consciousness.*

Each time I swore it was real—and it *was* real. A real disappointment. A real disaster. A real emptiness. I was less than a half, because I felt I couldn't even be a half.

But I thought about what Oscar and Lynda had told me. If I didn't have a boy, at least I had plenty of stories about boys. And honestly? Some of the stories were better than the boys themselves.

So, I thought, what could I do with these stories? Some people have poetry, or comics, or movies to make. Me? When I thought about it—really thought about it—I had songs.

I started to think of life in terms of a musical—this musical. I started to lose myself in writing it. It was about my life, and it was becoming my life.

The ring of ex-boyfriends leaves the stage.

TINY:

I was feeling low. And then I found something interesting:

Someone who was feeling even lower than I was.

A spotlight goes on and we see **WILL**, *nearly catatonic on a curb. (If you can't get a curb, a turned-over milk crate will do.) He is small and sad and clearly in pain.*

Do not underestimate the attractiveness of this. Nellie Forbush, Anna Leonowens, and Maria von Trapp all fell for it. Granted, they all fell for widowers. But Will was like a teenage version of a widower—only it was his own life he was mourning. Something about that made me want to swoop in and make everything better, adopt his children, save his homeland. (Metaphorically on those last two.)

Back to the action onstage. Tiny walks over and considers Will for a second. Will doesn't even notice . . . until Tiny speaks up.

TINY:

Hello there. I'm Tiny.

Tiny offers his hand. Will isn't in a shaking mood, but he holds out his hand, too. Instead of shaking it, Tiny yanks him up to his feet. Because that's what Will needs.

TINY:

Did someone die?

WILL:

Yeah, I did.

TINY:

Well, then . . . welcome to the afterlife.

Tiny turns to the audience for some exposition.

TINY (*to audience*):

Something really awful had just happened to

Will. I'm not going to tell you what, because that's his story, not mine. What's important is that he needed someone—and I guess I needed to be someone's someone. Even though he was a near-total stranger, I wanted to be there for him.

Tiny turns back to Will. And let me be clear here: Will is NOT into it. To a degree that Tiny doesn't even come close to realizing. Because in Tiny's mind, this is how things work—you meet cute, you stay cute, and you love cutely forever and ever, amen.

WILL:

You don't have to stay with me. Really. I'm sure you have better things to do.

TINY:

What, and leave you here to mope?

WILL:

This is so far beyond moping. This is out-and-out despair.

TINY:

Awwww.

You may ask what's going through Tiny's mind right now. I know I asked myself that many times afterward. Here is this desperate, depressed boy, and all Tiny can see is how much he needs love. One of the great things about being large-bodied is you can believe you can bend a situation through sheer physical will, that your embrace has more power than, say, a twig like Will's.

Tiny embraces Will in a big-ass hug.

WILL (*choking*):

I'm choking.

TINY (*patting his hair*):

There, there.

WILL (*pushing Tiny away*):

Dude, you're not helping.

TINY (*hurt*):

You just duded me!

WILL:

I'm sorry. It's just, I—

TINY:

I'm only trying to help!

WILL:

I'm sorry.

Tiny looks at Will, takes in all of his pain. It makes Will completely uncomfortable.

WILL:

What?

TINY:

Do you want to hear a song I've written?

WILL:

Excuse me?

TINY:

It's from a musical I'm working on. It's based on my life. I think one of the songs might help right now.

There is this amazing scene at the end of the first act of Once *when Guy gets on top of the bar and starts to play "Gold." The crowd is hostile at first, but one by one, they start playing instruments and dancing, and soon the whole stage is alive with music, as Girl wanders among the crowd, her face beaming with awestruck wonder at the remarkable thing that this song is doing. It's a perfect picture of what we musical devotees believe—that the right song at the right time can stop all the clocks, wipe away all the cares, and gently make you see the world in a new way. We believe this because we have felt it. We believe this because ultimately this is what we have to offer. Music. Words. Songs. A little light choreography.*

It may seem ridiculous for Tiny to burst out into song here. Will certainly finds it ridiculous. But in Tiny's heart, it makes perfect sense.

Tiny closes his eyes, opens his arms, and belts out **"IT WASN'T YOU."** *He is full of all the injustice that he's suffered at the hands of thoughtless ex-boyfriends. And he assumes this is why Will is feeling so bad, too. Plus, he's trying to impress the guy.*

["IT WASN'T YOU"]

TINY:

I thought you'd make my dreams come true
but it wasn't you, it wasn't you.

I thought this time it would all be new,
but it wasn't you, it wasn't you.

I pictured all the things we'd do
and now I feel my heart is through—
but it isn't true, it isn't true.

I may be big-boned and afraid
but my faith in love won't be mislaid!

Though I've been completely knocked off course
I'm not getting off my faithful horse!

It wasn't you, it's true
but there's more to life than you!

I thought you were a boy with a view,
you stuck-up, selfish, addled shrew.
You may have kicked me 'til I was blue
but from that experience I grew and grew.

It's true, frock you,
there are better guys to woo—
it won't be you, *comprende vous*?
It will never be you!

At the end, Tiny expects applause. And hopefully he gets some from the audience. But Will? Will stares at him, stunned.

WILL:

Who *are* you?

TINY:

Tiny Cooper!

WILL:

You can't really be named Tiny.

TINY:

No. That's irony.

WILL:

Oh.

TINY (*tsking*):

No need to "oh" me. I'm fine with it. I'm big-boned.

WILL:

Dude, it isn't just your bones.

TINY:

Just means there's more of me to love!

WILL:

But that requires so much more effort.

TINY:

Darling, I'm worth it.

Tiny gestures to a bench that has mysteriously appeared onstage. (Okay, maybe the audience will see that it's brought onto the stage at this moment. That's okay.) Tiny gestures for them to sit. They do.

TINY:

So tell Tiny your problems.

WILL:

Can Tiny talk normal?

TINY (*in his best Anderson Cooper voice*):
Yes, he can. But it's not nearly as fun when he does it.

WILL:
You just sound so gay.

TINY:
Um . . . there's a reason for that?

WILL:
Yeah, but. I dunno. I don't like gay people.

TINY:
But surely you must like yourself?

WILL (*incredulous*):
Why should I like myself? Nobody else does.

TINY:
I do.

WILL:
You don't know me at all.

TINY:
But I want to.

WILL (*freaking out*):
Shut up! Just shut up!

Tiny looks hurt. Which is a very understandable reaction to such an outburst.

WILL:

No, it's not you. Okay? You're nice. I'm not. I'm not nice, okay? Stop it!

Now Tiny is sad for Will. Because Will honestly believes this.

WILL:

This is SO STUPID.

Will clutches at his head while he cries this out, like he feels he is going completely out of his mind. For once in his life, Tiny is the steady one. He just watches Will, waits. And the longer he watches, the more he cares. When Will finally lifts his head and stops being angry at himself, they hang in a strange, intimate moment.

TINY:

I never kiss on the first date.

Will looks at him with total incomprehension.

TINY:

But sometimes I make exceptions.

It's as if gravity conspires to push them toward each other. They kiss, eyes closed. When they're done, Tiny looks happy and Will looks scared.

TINY:

This is not where I thought the night was going.

WILL:

Tell me about it. (*His tone softens.*) But . . . I'm glad that you exist.

TINY:

I'm glad to be existing right now.

WILL:

You have no idea how wrong you are about me.

TINY:

You have no idea how wrong you are about yourself.

WILL:

Stop that.

TINY:

Only if you stop it.

WILL:

I'm warning you.

TINY

(*standing from the bench, ending the scene, and addressing the audience*):

Of course, when a boy gives you a warning, you should listen to it. Not because he's necessarily right. But because he genuinely thinks he is. And most of the time, that's more important.

Will leaves the stage. Phil and Djane enter, and Tiny flags them down.

TINY:

Guys! I've got so much to tell you!

ACT II, SCENE 10

Tiny is very, very excited about Will. As a result, he babbles uncontrollably to Phil and Djane. **"DRUNK ON LOVE"** *is their take on this situation—and a resolution to the unbearable sexual tension between them that their friends have been enduring for* weeks. *Tiny should basically be talking the whole time, with his voice fading out as Phil and Djane sing. When he talks, he should sound very, very drunk. In parts where he doesn't want to talk, he can also do a happy This Fella's in Love dance. He should seem completely intoxicated by this new relationship—soon to be the most serious one he's ever had.*

["DRUNK ON LOVE"]

TINY (*spoken drunkenly*):
So I'm sorry I didn't go back to Frenchy's to meet you, but I figured you'd guess I just took a cab, which I did, and anyway, Will and I had walked all the way down to the Bean and, like, Wrayson, I know I've said this before but I *really like him.* I mean, you have to *really* like someone to go all the way to the Bean with him and listen to him talk about his major major problems and also I *sang* for him . . .

DJANE (*sung to* **PHIL**):
Oh my God, who would've thunk?

PHIL (*sung back*):

Our dear friend Tiny is drunk . . . on love.

DJANE:

Get the Breathalyzer
and cue the synthesizer!
Our dear friend Tiny is drunk . . . on love.

TINY:

And I get texts from him like every forty-two seconds and he's a brilliant texter, which is nice because it's just a little pleasant leg vibration, just a reminder-in-the-thigh that he's—see, there's one. (*checks phone*) *Aww.*

PHIL:

It looks like our pal is out of his funk.

DJANE:

Tiny Cooper, drunk . . . on love.

PHIL:

His spirits are higher
than those of a frequent flier.
Tiny Cooper, drunk . . . on love

TINY:

It's been eight days since I met him, and I haven't technically liked someone who liked me back for eight days in my entire life, unless you count my relationship with Bethany Keene in third grade, which obviously you can't, since she's a girl.

PHIL:

Good ol' Bacchus
needs in on this fracas.

DJANE:

Aphrodite's throwing a fest
and Tiny's the honored guest.

PHIL:

Look at him frolic.
Look at him skip.
It makes me wonder
if *we* should sip.

The music abruptly stops. Tiny stops. Djane stares. Did Phil really just do what she thinks he just did?

DJANE (*spoken*):

Did you really just do what I think you just did?

PHIL

(*continuing the song, moving closer to Djane*):

I'm not promising you

it'll be a slam dunk,
but, Djane, I'm thinking
we should get a little drunk.
Uncork the bottle and
drown the monk.
We won't know if it's sink or swim
'til we've swum or sunk.

DJANE (*moving even closer*):
You know what I have to say to that?

PHIL
(*even closer—they both kinda know what's coming*):
What?

An explosive kiss between them. It's impossible to tell who kissed who first.

They take it offstage.

TINY (*to audience*):
Now, *that's* what I'm talking about. And that's what Will and I had. Only, we had other things, too. Like fear. And vulnerability. And uncertainty. I tried to shine my way through all these things . . . shine us both through all these things. But sometimes it's not that easy.

The bed gets wheeled in again, with different sheets on it. We're in Will's bedroom now. It's very much like the inside of his head—part childish, part intense. Although the sheets weren't actually black, they might as well have been.

Will and Tiny have been dating for a couple of weeks now. Tiny is SO into it, and he feels that Will is, too, even if Will isn't as open in expressing his enthusiasm. But that's okay. Tiny has learned to understand that his emotional volume tends to be a little louder than other boys', and he wants Will to be his complement, not his twin. It's okay that they're different, in no small part because Tiny thinks his buoyancy can lift whatever's weighing Will down. They'll balance out.

Will enters the bedroom and joins Tiny.

TINY (*to audience*):

This is the first time I ever got to see Will's room. You can tell a lot about a guy from his room. In Will's case, I was searching for signs of life.

Tiny approaches a goldfish bowl next to the bed. You do NOT have to have goldfish in it. This is acting. And no goldfish should have to swim under a spotlight.

TINY:

Goldfish! What are their names?

WILL:

Samson and Delilah.

TINY:

Really?

WILL:

She's a total slut.

Tiny leans over for a closer look at the fish food and finds a bottle of pills instead.

TINY:

You feed them prescription drugs?

WILL:

Oh, no. Those are mine. (*pause*) It's a depression thing.

TINY (*lighthearted, not really getting it*):

Oh, I feel depressed, too. Sometimes. (*pause*) Which one's Samson and which one's Delilah?

WILL:

Honestly? I forget.

TINY (*as if he's just seen it for the first time*):

Look! A bed!

With an almost-shy grin, Tiny sits gingerly on its edge.

TINY:

Comfy!

Will takes one look at Tiny sitting there and laughs happily. It's a wonderful sound when he laughs happily, especially because it surprises Will whenever it happens.

TINY:

What?

WILL:

There's a boy! In my bed!

Will joins Tiny in the bed. They share a tender kiss, then Will lies in Tiny's arms. It's very sweet. And I wish we could end the scene here. With all my heart, I wish we could end the scene here, and Will could let this be exactly what it seems to be. But Will can't accept it. He pulls out of Tiny's embrace, sits up.

TINY:

What? What is it?

WILL:

Look, Tiny—I'm trying to be on my best behavior, but you have to understand—I'm always standing on the edge of something bad. And sometimes someone like you can make me look the other way, so that I don't know how close I am to falling over. But I always end up turning my head. Always. I always walk off that edge. And it's what I deal with every day, and it's not going away anytime soon. It's really nice to have you here, but do you want to know something? Do you really want me to be honest?

Tiny nods. Of course he wants Will to be honest. When you're falling in love, you always think honesty is the right answer.

WILL:

It feels like a vacation. I don't think you know what that's like. Which is good—you don't want to. You have no idea how much I hate this. I hate the fact that I'm ruining the night right now, ruining everything—

TINY:

You're not.

WILL:

I am.

TINY:

Says who?

WILL:

Says me?

TINY:

Don't I get any say?

WILL:

No. I just ruin it. You don't get any say.

Tiny touches Will's ear lightly, tries to lighten the moment.

TINY:

You know, you get all sexy when you turn destructive.

His fingers run down Will's neck, under his collar.

TINY:

I know I can't change anything that's already happened to you. But you know what I can do?

WILL:

What?

TINY:

Something else. That's what I can give you.
Something else.

The next song is a ballad, almost a lullaby, delivered from Tiny to Will as Tiny cuddles him close. Tiny wants so badly for Will to see how much he cares. As happens with love, he cares carefully, and he cares carelessly, and he cares a lot about how much his care is received. He sees Will is hurting. He knows *Will is hurting. And he wants to change that. And he believes that the first step to change is letting the other person know that you're there, and that you want to help as much as he needs help.*

I wanted to be his escape plan. I thought I could write it myself.

["SOMETHING ELSE"]

TINY:

If you're tired of feeling,
tired of fighting,
I understand.

If you're tired of twisting,
exhausted by existing,
I understand.

Sometimes it takes all your strength
to get up in the morning,

only to face a day
that seems aimless and boring.

But don't despair
because I'll be there
to lead you away.

I'll be your weekend,
your fire escape,
the dream you never leave—

I'll be your day off,
your stopped clock,
your glorious reprieve.

Let me be your something else.
Let me put your past up on a shelf.
Let me unfold you from your problems
and let you be yourself.

If you're tired of the mess,
tired of the stress,
I understand.

If you're tired of every thought,
sick of feeling caught,
I understand.

Sometimes it takes all of your strength
to make it through the night,

only to wake up
and find little that feels right.

But don't despair
because I'll be there
to lead you away.

I'll be your weekend,
your fire escape,
the dream you never leave—

I'll be your day off,
your stopped clock,
your glorious reprieve.

Let me be your something else.
Let me put your past up on a shelf.
Let me unfold you from your problems
and let you be yourself.

Just come away with me.
Come away with me.
Put all the rest of it aside
and come away with me.
We all miss our heavens
and we all fight our hells.
So please let me be there
to be your something else.

The end of the song lulls them together. It's almost possible to believe they've made it to something else. It's almost possible to believe they've made it to where they need to be.

This is hard to write. Please know this is hard to write.

Lights out.

ACT II, SCENE 11

A few more weeks pass. If you ask Tiny, he'll tell you he's never been happier. But every time he says this, every time he proclaims *it, there's a little piece that feels hollow.*

There's a lot he's trying to balance. His relationship with Will. The creation of this musical. Phil Wrayson's ongoing drama/comedy with Djane.

There isn't much time to think about love. And of course that means it's all he thinks about.

TINY:

Miracles and curses. Curses and miracles. It's the same magic, played different ways.

So it is with love. Or our attempt at love. The exhilaration and the disappointment. The quiet and the noise. The passionate disagreement and the passionate agreement. The same magic, played different ways.

There's a reason that, when we remember relationships, most of the time the most intense memories are from the beginning or the end. Because that's when we're most aware of the magic. Positive, negative. Rise, fall.

There were times while I was writing this musical over the past few weeks that I thought it might have a happy ending. I thought I was writing about me at first, then I realized I was writing about love. I thought I could give both of us a happy ending.

But it's not so simple.

A few days ago, I said something to one of Will's former friends that maybe I shouldn't have. I'm sorry about it, but I wasn't sorry about it quick enough. Again, I'm not going to go into it, because that's his story and not mine.

It's not a happy ending, but I'm not convinced it's a sad one either.

Some things end. Some things stay.

We're going to start the scene with Will madder at me than he's ever been.

Will storms onto the stage, angry and distressed. He and Tiny plunge right into the fight. Like most couples' fights, it starts being about one thing, but soon becomes about a lot more.

WILL:

You really shouldn't have done that.

TINY:

Why?

WILL:

Why? Because it's my life, my problem. And you can't fix it. When you try, it only makes it worse.

TINY:

Stop it.

WILL:

Stop what?

TINY:

Stop talking to me like I'm stupid. I'm not stupid.

WILL:

I know you're not stupid. But you sure as hell did a stupid thing.

TINY:

This isn't how the day was supposed to go.

WILL:

Well, you know what? A lot of the time, you have no control over how your day goes.

TINY:

Stop. Please. I want this to be a nice day. Let's go somewhere you like to go. Where should we go? Take me somewhere that matters to you.

WILL:

Like what?

TINY:

Like . . . I don't know. For me, if I need to feel better, I go alone to Super Target. I don't know why, but seeing all of those things makes me happy. It's probably the design. I don't even have to buy anything. Just seeing all the people together, seeing all the things I *could* buy—all the colors, aisle after aisle—sometimes I need that. For Djane, it's this indie record store we'll go to so she can look at old vinyl while I look at all the boy band CDs in the two-dollar bin and try to figure out which one I think is the cutest. Or for Phil there's this park in our town, where all the Little League teams play. And he loves the dugout, because when no one else is around, it's really quiet there. When there's not a game on, you can sit there and all that exists are the things that happened in the past. I think everyone has a place like that. You must have a place like that.

WILL (*shaking his head*):

Nothing.

TINY:

C'mon. There has to be someplace.

WILL:

There isn't, okay? Just my house. My room. That's it.

TINY:

Fine—then where's the nearest swing set?

The swing set from the opening of Act II is returned to the stage.

TINY:

Here's one!

Tiny sits on one of the swings.

TINY:

Join me. (*Will does.*) Now, isn't this better?

WILL:

Better than what?

Tiny laughs and shakes his head.

WILL:

What? Why are you shaking your head?

TINY:

It's nothing.

WILL:

Tell me.

TINY:

It's just funny.

WILL:

What's funny?

TINY:

You. And me.

WILL:

I'm glad you find it funny.

TINY:

I wish you'd find it funnier. (*pause*) You know what's a great metaphor for love?

WILL:

I have a feeling you're about to tell me.

Tiny turns away and makes an attempt to swing high. The swing set groans so much that he stops and twists back Will's way.

TINY:

Sleeping Beauty.

WILL:

Sleeping Beauty?

TINY:

Yes, because you have to plow through this incredible thicket of thorns in order to get to Beauty, and even then, when you get there, you still have to wake her up.

WILL:

So I'm a thicket?

TINY:

And the beauty that isn't full awake yet.

WILL:

It figures you'd think that way.

TINY:

Why?

WILL:

Well, your life is a musical. Literally.

TINY:

Do you hear me singing now?

There's a silence as they swing.

WILL:

Tiny . . .

TINY:

Will . . .

WILL:

Don't you get it? I don't need anyone.

TINY:

That only means you need me more.

WILL:

You're not in love with me. You're in love with my need.

TINY:

But I like you. I really, really like you.

WILL:

I'm really sorry.

Tiny swings for a moment.

TINY:

Don't be. I fell for you. I know what happens at the end of falling—landing.

WILL:

I just get so pissed off at myself. I'm the worst thing in the world for you. I'm your pinless hand grenade.

TINY:

I like my pinless hand grenade.

WILL:

Well, I don't like being your pinless hand grenade. Or anybody's.

TINY:

I just want you to be happy. If that's with me or with someone else or with nobody. I just want you to be happy. I just want you to be okay with life. With life as it is. And me, too. It is so hard to accept that life is falling. Falling and landing and falling and landing. I agree it's not ideal. I agree.

But there is the word, this word Phil Wrayson taught me once: *weltschmerz*. It's the depression you feel when the world as it is does not line up with the world as you think it should be. I live in a big goddamned *weltschmerz* ocean, you know? And so do you. And so does everyone. Because everyone thinks it should be possible just to keep falling and falling forever, to feel the rush of the air on your face as you fall, that air pulling your face into a brilliant goddamned smile. And that *should* be possible. You *should* be able to fall forever.

You're still a pinless grenade over the world not being perfect. And I'm still—every time this happens to me, every time I land, it still hurts like it's never happened before.

Tiny's swinging higher now, kicking his legs hard, the swing set groaning. It looks like he's going to bring the whole contraption down, but he just keeps pumping his legs and pulling against the chain with his arms and talking.

TINY:

Because we can't stop the *weltschmerz*. We can't stop imagining the world as it might be. Which is awesome! It is my favorite thing about us!

And if you're gonna have that, you're gonna have falling. They don't call it *rising* in love. That's why I love us!

Because we know what will happen when we fall!

Tiny leaps from the swing . . . and this time lands on his feet. As soon as he does, the finale begins.

["FINALE"]

TINY:

It's all about falling—
you land and get up so you can fall again.
It's all about falling—
I won't be afraid to hit that wall again.

I like love.
There, I've said it:
I really like love.
Not as a half
but as a whole
looking for another whole.

I want to be like my mom and dad—
I want to feel the love they've had.
I want to share this love with all my friends—
I want to fall alongside them 'til our story ends.

I was born big-boned and happily gay
but I've learned so much more along the way.

MOM and DAD:

In the cold
In the wind
We'll be there for you.

Your agony
Your ecstasy
We will feel it.

MOM:

The strongest kind of love
is unconditional love.
The moment you were born,
I knew unconditional love.

DAD:

In so many ways you amaze me.

MOM:

In so many ways you amaze me.

LYNDA and THE GHOST OF OSCAR WILDE:

Look forward to the moment
when it falls apart.
Look forward to the moment
when you must rearrange your heart.

It might feel like the end of the world—
but it's the beginning of your art.

PHIL and DJANE:

We hope you can you abide
us showing some Tiny Cooper pride.
Hold me closer, Tiny Cooper!
Hold me closer, Tiny Cooper!
Even as you fall,
hold me closer.

CHORUS OF EX-BOYFRIENDS:

It's all about falling—
you land and get up so you can fall again.
It's all about falling—
I won't be afraid to hit that wall again.

TINY (*spoken*):

Maybe tonight you're scared of falling, and maybe there's somebody here or somewhere else you're thinking about, worrying over, fretting over, trying to figure out if you want to fall, or how and when you're gonna land, and I gotta tell you, friends, to stop thinking about the landing, because it's all about falling.

Maybe there is something you're afraid to say, or someone you're afraid to love, or somewhere you're afraid to go. It's gonna hurt. It's gonna hurt because it matters.

CHORUS:

Don't be afraid—

just fall.
Don't be afraid—
just fall.

TINY:

But I just fell and landed and I am still standing here to tell you that you've gotta learn to love the falling, because it's all about falling.

CHORUS:

Don't be afraid—
just fall.
Don't be afraid—
just fall.

TINY:

Just fall for once. Let yourself fall!

Everybody should be onstage now. The whole ensemble. Singing together. Ex-boyfriends and friends. Members of the family I was born into and members of the family I've created. This one big chorus that sings me through my life, adding the harmony that makes me awake and alive and connected. In this moment I realize: I don't need that one single other voice to make my life a song. There are so many voices that are already a part of it. We diminuendo in our doubt, but then we crescendo into understanding, together.

ENSEMBLE:

Hold me closer,
hold me closer.
Hold me closer,
hold me closer!

I'm going to fall,
so hold me closer!
I'm going to fall,
so hold me closer!

Every time I fall,
hold me closer.
Every time I fall,
hold me closer!

Suddenly, with a grand wave of his arms, Tiny stops the music. He moves to the front of the stage and the rest of the stage goes dark. It's just him in a spotlight, looking out into the audience. He just stands there for a moment, taking it all in. And then he closes the show by saying:

TINY:

My name is Tiny Cooper. And this is my story.

With this, our show comes to an end. It's an open ending, and it's a happy ending. Because most happy endings are open endings—wide-open endings. On opening night of this musical, a lot of things happened to make me realize that life is a work in progress, and that we're actors and playwrights and composers, if we approach the show the right way. This is my first show, and I'm sure it's rough—most first shows are. But it won't be my last.

I have to believe we have enough songs in our hearts for endless musicals, about an endless number of things. And it's fun, every now and then, to let them out into the world.

Thank you for hearing me.

FIN

Tiny Cooper would like to thank:

All of the exes who taught him something, particularly Will.

His parents, for being awesome.

Will (not the same as the Will above), for being a best friend even when it was hard to be a best friend, because that's what being a best friend's about.

Jane, for helping to contain my wilder thoughts.

My actors, for being subject to my wilder thoughts.

Chance, for being there in the audience on opening night, and giving me his phone number. It's amazing what's happened since.

Most of all, thanks to anyone who's shown me appreciation. Believe me, it is appreciated in return.

David Levithan would like to thank:

John, for co-parenting Tiny, and for always being supportive of this crazy musical endeavor.

My parents, for being awesome.

Chris, for letting me run through the first act when we were in Costa Rica.

Billy, Nick, and Zack, for letting me run through the first draft when we were in Hilton Head.

Collin, for spending some of his first summer in New York reading this.

Hunter, for his musical expertise and his super-friendly encouragement.

Eliot, for helping out right before the curtain went up.

Libba, Nova, and Justin, for Monday-morning check-ins.

All my other author friends, for making this such a damn great community. And to readers, for making a damn great community of their own.

Julie, Melissa, Lauren, and everyone at Penguin USA, Ben and everyone at Penguin UK, Michael and Penny and everyone at Text, and Bill, Chris, and Alicia, for helping Tiny to sing.

Most of all, thanks to anyone who's shown me appreciation. Believe me, it is appreciated in return.

For more about this musical, go to
www.davidlevithan.com/holdmecloser

Turn the page for a sample of the novel that introduced Tiny Cooper to the world—

chapter two

i am constantly torn between killing myself and killing everyone around me.

those seem to be the two choices. everything else is just killing time.

right now i'm walking through the kitchen to get to the back door.

mom: have some breakfast.

i do not eat breakfast. i never eat breakfast. i haven't eaten breakfast since i was able to walk out the back door without eating breakfast first.

mom: where are you going?

school, mom. you should try it some time.

mom: don't let your hair fall in your face like that – i can't see your eyes.

but you see, mom, that's *the whole fucking point.*

i feel bad for her – i do. a damn shame, really, that i had to have a mother. it can't be easy having me for a son. nothing can prepare someone for that kind of disappointment.

me: bye

i do not say 'good-bye.' i believe that's one of the bullshittiest words ever invented. it's not like you're given the choice to say 'bad-bye' or 'awful-bye' or 'couldn't-care-less-about-you-bye.' every time you leave, it's supposed to be a good one. well, i don't believe in that. i believe *against* that.

mom: have a good d—

the door kinda closes in the middle of her sentence, but it's not like i can't guess where it's going. she used to say 'see you!' until one morning i was so sick of it i told her, 'no, you don't.'

she tries, and that's what makes it so pathetic. i just want to say, 'i feel sorry for you, really i do.' but that might start a conversation, and a conversation might start a fight, and then i'd feel so guilty i might have to move away to portland or something.

i need coffee.

every morning i pray that the school bus will crash and we'll all die in a fiery wreck. then my mom will be able to sue the school bus company for never making school buses with seat belts, and she'll be able to get more money for my tragic death than i would've ever made in my tragic life. unless the lawyers from the school bus company can prove to the jury that i was guaranteed to be a fuckup. then they'd get away with buying my mom a used ford fiesta and calling it even.

maura isn't exactly waiting for me before school, but i know, and she knows i'll look for her where she is. we usually fall back on that so we can smirk at each other or something before we're marched off. it's like those people who become friends in prison even though they would never really talk to each other if they weren't in prison. that's what maura and i are like, i think.

me: give me some coffee.
maura: get your own fucking coffee.

then she hands me her XXL dunkin donuts crappaccino and i treat it like it's a big gulp. if i could afford my own coffee i swear i'd get it, but the way i see it is: her bladder isn't thinking i'm an asshole even if the rest of her organs do. it's been like this with me and maura for as long as I can remember, which is about a year. i guess i've known her a little longer than that, but maybe not. at some point last year, her gloom met my doom and she thought it was a good match. i'm not so sure, but at least i get coffee out of it.

derek and simon are coming over now, which is good because it's going to save me some time at lunch.

me: give me your math homework.
simon: sure. here.

what a friend.

the first bell rings. like all the bells in our fine institution of lower learning, it's not a bell at all, it's a long beep, like you're about to leave a voicemail saying you're having the suckiest day ever. and nobody's ever going to listen to it.

i have no idea why anyone would want to become a teacher. i mean, you have to spend the day with a group of kids who either hate your guts or are kissing up to you to get a good grade. that has to get to you after a while, being surrounded by people who will never like you for any real reason. i'd feel bad for them if they weren't such sadists and losers. with the sadists, it's all about the power and the control. they teach so they can have an official reason to dominate other people. and the losers make up pretty much all the other teachers, from the ones who are too incompetent to do anything else to the ones who want to be their students' best friends because they never had friends when they were in high school. and there are the ones who honestly think we're going to remember a thing they say to us after final exams are over. right.

every now and then you get a teacher like mrs. grover, who's a sadistic loser. i mean, it can't be easy being a french teacher, because nobody really needs to know how to speak french anymore. and while she kisses the honors kids' *derrieres,* with standard kids she resents the fact that we're taking up her time. so she responds by giving us quizzes every day and giving us gay projects like 'design your own ride for euro disney' and then acting all surprised when i'm like 'yeah, my ride for euro disney is minnie using a baguette as a dildo to have some fun with mickey.' since i don't have any idea how to say 'dildo' in french (*dildot?*), i just say 'dildo' and she pretends to have no idea what i'm talking about and says that minnie and mickey eating baguettes isn't a ride. no doubt she gives me a check-minus for the day. i know i'm supposed to care, but really it's hard to imagine something i could care less about than my grade in french.

the only worthwhile thing i do all period – all morning, really – is write *isaac, isaac, isaac* in my notebook and then draw spider-man spelling it out in a web. which is completely lame, but whatever. it's not like i'm doing it to be cool.

i sit with derek and simon at lunch. the way it is with us, it's like we're sitting in a waiting room. every now and then we'll say something, but mostly we stick to our own chair-sized spaces. occasionally we'll read magazines. if someone comes over, we'll look up. but that doesn't happen often.

we ignore most of the people who walk by, even the ones we're supposed to lust after. it's not like derek and simon are into girls. basically, they like computers.

derek: do you think the X18 software will be released before summer?

simon: i read on trustmaster's blog that it might. that would be cool.

me: here's your homework back.

when i look at the guys and girls at the other tables, i wonder what they could possibly have to say to each other. they're all so boring and they're all trying to make up for it by talking louder. i'd rather just sit here and eat.

i have this ritual, that when it hits two o'clock i allow myself to get excited about leaving. it's like if i reach that point i can take the rest of the day off.

it happens in math, and maura is sitting next to me. she figured out in october what i was doing, so now every day at two she passes me a slip of paper with something on it. like 'congratulations' or 'can we go now?' or 'if this period doesn't end soon i am going to slit my own skull.' i know i should write her back, but mostly i nod. i think she wants us to go out on a date or something, and i don't know what to do about that.

everyone in our school has afterschool activities.

mine is going home.

sometimes i stop and board for a while in the park, but not in february, not in this witch-twat-frigid chicago suburb (known to locals as naperville). if i go out there now, i'll freeze my balls off. not that i'm putting them to any use whatsoever, but i still like to have them, just in case.

plus i've got better things to do than have the college dropouts tell me when i can ramp (usually about . . . never) and have the skatepunks from our school look down at me because i'm not cool enough to smoke and drink with them and i'm not cool enough to be straightedge. i'm no-edge as far as they're concerned. i stopped trying to be in their in-crowd-that-doesn't-admit-it's-an-in-crowd when i left ninth grade. it's not like boarding is my life or anything.

i like having the house to myself when i get home. i don't have to feel guilty about ignoring my mom if she's not around.

i head to the computer first and see if isaac's online. he's not, so i fix myself a cheese sandwich (i'm too lazy to grill it) and jerk off. it takes about ten minutes, but it's not like i'm timing it.

isaac's still not on when i get back. he's the only person on my 'buddy list,' which is the stupidest fucking name for a list. what are we, three years old?

me: hey, isaac, wanna be my buddy!?
isaac: sure, buddy! let's go *fishin'*!

isaac knows how stupid i find these things, and he finds them just as stupid as i do. like lol. now, if there's anything stupider than buddy lists, it's lol. if anyone ever uses lol with me, i rip my computer right out of the wall and smash it over the nearest head. i mean, it's not like anyone is laughing out loud about the things they lol. i think it should be spelled loll, like what a lobotomized person's tongue does. loll. loll. i can't think any more. loll. loll!

or ttyl. bitch, you're not actually *talking*. that would require actual *vocal contact*. or <3. you think that looks like a heart? if you do, that's only because you've never seen scrotum.

(rofl! what? are you really rolling on the floor laughing? well, please stay down there a sec while I KICK YOUR ASS.)

i had to tell maura that my mom made me get rid of my instant messenger in order for her to stop popping up whenever i was trying to do something.

gothblood4567: 'sup?
finalwill: i'm working.
gothblood4567: on what?
finalwill: my suicide note. i can't figure out how to end it.
gothblood4567: lol

so i killed my screenname and resurrected myself under another. isaac's the only person who knows it, and it's going to stay that way.

i check my email and it's mostly spam. what i want to know is this: is there really someone in the whole world who gets an email from hlyywkrrs@hothotmail.com, reads it, and says to himself, 'you know, what i really need to do is enlarge my penis 33%, and the way to do it would be to send $69.99 to that nice lady ilena at VIRILITY MAXIMUS CORP via this handy internet link!' if people are actually falling for that, it's not their dicks they should be worried about.

i have a friend request from some stranger on facebook and i delete it without looking at the profile because that doesn't seem natural. 'cause friendship should not be as easy as that. it's like people believe all you need to do is like the same bands in order to be soulmates. or books. *omg . . . U like the outsiders 2 . . . it's like we're the same person!* no we're not. it's like we have the same english teacher. there's a difference.

it's almost four and isaac's usually on by now. i do that stupid reward thing with my homework – it's like *if i look up what date the mayans invented toothpicks, i can check to see if isaac's online yet.* then *if i read three more paragraphs about the importance of pottery in indigenous cultures, i can check my yahoo account.* and finally *if i finish answering all three of these questions and isaac isn't on yet, then i can jerk off again.*

i'm only halfway through answering the first question, some bullshit about why mayan pyramids are *so much cooler* than egyptian ones, when i cheat and look at my buddy list and see that isaac's name is there. i'm about to think *why hasn't he IM'ed me?* when the box appears on the screen. like he's read my mind.

boundbydad: u there?
grayscale: yes!
boundbydad: ☺
grayscale: ☺ x 100
boundbydad: i've been thinking about you all day
grayscale: ???
boundbydad: only good things
grayscale: that's too bad ☺
boundbydad: depends on what you think of as good ☺☺

it's been like this from the beginning. just being comfortable. i was a little freaked out at first by his screenname, but he quickly told me it was because his name was isaac, and ultimatelymydadchosetokillthegoatinsteadofme was too long to be a good screenname. he asked me about my old screenname, finalwill, and i told him my name was will, and that's how we started to get to know each other. we were in one of those lame chatrooms where it falls completely silent every ten seconds until someone goes 'anyone in here?' and other people are like 'yeah' 'yup' 'here!' without saying anything. we were supposed to be in a forum for this singer i used to like, but there wasn't much to say about him except which songs were better than the other songs. it was really boring, but it's how isaac and i met, so i guess we'll have to hire the singer to play at our wedding or something. (that is so not funny.)

soon we were swapping pictures and mp3s and telling each other about how everything pretty much sucked, but of course the ironic part was that while we were talking about it the world didn't suck as much. except, of course, for the part at the end when we had to return to the real world.

it is so unfair that he lives in ohio, because that should be close enough, but since neither of us drives and neither of us would ever in a million years say, 'hey, mom, do you want to drive me across indiana to see a boy?,' we're kind of stuck.

grayscale: i'm reading about the mayans.
boundbydad: angelou?
grayscale: ???
boundbydad: nevermind. we skipped the mayans. we only read 'american' history now.
grayscale: but aren't they in the americas?

boundbydad: not according to my school. **groans**
grayscale: so who did you almost kill today?
grayscale: and by 'kill,' i mean 'wish would disappear,' just in case this conversation is being monitored by administrators
boundbydad: potential body count of eleven. twelve if you count the cat.
grayscale: . . . or homeland security
grayscale: goddamn cat!
boundbydad: goddamn cat!

i haven't told anyone about isaac because it's none of their business. i love that he knows who everyone is but nobody knows who he is. if i had actual friends that i felt i could talk to, this might cause some conflict. but since right now there'd only need to be one car to take people to my funeral, i think it's okay.

eventually isaac has to go, because he isn't really supposed to be using the computer at the music store where he works. lucky for me that it doesn't seem to be a busy music store, and his boss is like a drug dealer or something and is always leaving isaac in charge while he goes out to 'meet some people.'

i step away from the computer and finish my homework quickly. then i go in the den and turn on law & order, since the only thing i can really count on in life is that whenever i turn on the tv there will be a law & order episode. this time it's the one with the guy who strangles blonde after blonde after blonde, and even though i'm pretty sure i've seen it like ten times already, i'm watching it like i don't know that the pretty reporter he's talking to is about to have the curtain cord around her neck. i don't watch that part, because it's really stupid, but once the police catch the guy and the trial's going on, they're all

lawyer: dude, the cord knocked this microscopic piece of skin off your hand while you were strangling her, and we ran it under the microscope and found out that you're totally fucked.

you gotta know he wishes he'd worn gloves, although the gloves probably would've left fibers, and he would've been totally fucked anyway. when that's all over, there's another episode i don't think i've seen before, until this celebrity runs over a baby in his hummer and i'm like, oh, it's the one where the celebrity runs over the baby in his hummer. i watch it anyway, because it's not like i have anything better to do. then mom comes home and finds me there and it's like we're a rerun, too.

mom: how was your day?
me: mom, i'm watching tv.
mom: will you be ready for dinner in fifteen minutes?
me: *mom,* i'm watching tv!
mom: well, set the table during the commercials.
me: FINE.

i totally don't get this – is there anything more boring and pathetic than setting the table when there are only two of you? i mean, with place mats and salad forks and everything. who is she kidding? i would give anything not to have to spend the next twenty minutes sitting across from her, because she doesn't believe in letting silence go. no, she has to fill it up with talk. i want to tell her that's what the voices in your head are for, to get you through all the silent parts. but she doesn't want to be with her thoughts unless she's saying them out loud.

mom: if i get lucky tonight, maybe we'll have a few more dollars for the car fund.
me: you really don't need to do that.
mom: don't be silly. it gives me a reason to go to girls' poker night.

i really wish she would stop it. she feels worse about me not having a car than i do. i mean, i'm not one of those jerks who thinks that as soon as you turn seventeen it's your god-given american right to have a brand-new chevrolet in the driveway. i know what our situation is, and i know she doesn't like that i have to work weekends at cvs in order to afford the things we need to pick up at cvs. having her constantly sad about it doesn't make me feel better. and of course there's another reason for her to go play poker besides the money. she needs more friends.

she asks me if i took my pills before i ran off this morning and i tell her, yeah, wouldn't i be drowning myself in the bathtub if i hadn't? she doesn't like that, so i'm all like 'joke, joke' and i make a mental note that moms aren't the best audience for medication humor. i decide not to get her that *world's greatest mom of a depressive fuckup* sweatshirt for mother's day like i'd been planning. (okay, there's not really a sweatshirt like that, but if there was, it would have kittens on it, putting their paws in sockets.)

truth is, thinking about depression depresses the shit out of me, so i go back into the den and watch some more law & order. isaac's never back at his computer until eight, so i wait until then. maura calls me but i don't have the energy to say anything to her except what's happening on law & order, and she hates it when i do that. so i let the voicemail pick up.

me: this is will. why the fuck are you calling me? leave a message and maybe i'll call you back. [BEEP]

maura: hey, loser. i'm so bored i'm calling you. i figured if you weren't doing anything i could bear your children. oh, well. i guess i'll just go call joseph and ask him to do me in the manger and begat another holy child.

by the time i care, it's almost eight. and even then, i don't care enough to call her back. we have this thing about calling each other back, in that we don't do it very much. instead i head to the computer and it's like i turn into a little girl who's just seen her first rainbow. i get all giddy and nervous and hopeful and despairing and i tell myself not to look obsessively at my buddy list, but it might as well be projected onto the insides of my eyelids. at 8:05 his name pops up, and i start to count. i only get to twelve before his IM pops up.

boundbydad: greetings!

grayscale: and salutations!
boundbydad: so glad u're here.
grayscale: so glad to be here
boundbydad: work today = lamest! day! ever! this girl tried to shoplift and wasn't even subtle about it. i used to have some sympathy for shoplifters
boundbydad: but now i just want to see them behind bars. i told her to put it back and she acted all 'put what back?' until i reached into her pocket and took the disc out. and what does she say to that? 'oh.'
grayscale: not even 'sorry'?
boundbydad: not even.
grayscale: girls suck.
boundbydad: and boys are angels? ☺

we go on like this for about an hour. i wish we could talk on the phone, but his parents won't let him have a cell and i know my mom sometimes checks my phone log when i'm in the shower. this is nice, though. it's the only part of my day when the time actually seems worth it.